BONUS
STORY

KONOSUBA:
AN EXPLOSION
ON THIS WONDERFUL
WORLD!

We Are the
Megumin Bandits

Megumin

"My name is **Megumin!** She who leads a pure, just, and **respectable thief gang** who steals **for the sake of the world and its people!**"

"I'm Cecily, a distinguished and beautiful priestess of the Axis Church. Feel free to call me Big Sis."

Cecily

"I'm supposed to have good luck, right? Why do I keep ending up in these amusing situations...?"

Chris

"By all means, let me in! Let me join the two of you!"

Iris

"I don't know what you're gonna do—I just thought I'd like to be a part of it..."

Yunyun

"No, Megumin! We only recently started thieving together, and I told you before—I don't think anything of my lowly assistant! He's just a friend; I don't have any special feelings!"

"Wait a second— what have the two of you been talking about behind my back? Why have I been rejected without even knowing about it?"

🔥 Kazuma

"Er, are you guys really close? How long have you two had this kind of relationship?"

CONTENTS

BONUS STORY

KONOSUBA: AN EXPLOSION ON THIS WONDERFUL WORLD! We Are the Megumin Bandits

Illustrations / Kurone Mishima

Design / Yuuko Mukadeya + Kaiko Monma (Mushikago Graphics)

KONOSUBA: BONUS STORY
AN EXPLOSION ON THIS WONDERFUL WORLD!

1

We Are the Megumin Bandits

NATSUME AKATSUKI

ILLUSTRATION BY
KURONE MISHIMA

YEN
ON
NEW YORK

KONOSUBA: AN EXPLOSION ON THIS WONDERFUL WORLD! 1 BONUS STORY

NATSUME AKATSUKI

Translation by Alex Wetnight
Cover art by Kurone Mishima

KONO SUBARASHII SEKAI NI SHUKUFUKU WO! SPIN OFF ZOKU · KONO SUBARASHII SEKAI NI BAKUEN WO! Vol. 1
WARERA, MEGUMIN TOUZOKUDAN
©Natsume Akatsuki, Kurone Mishima 2016
First published in Japan in 2016 by KADOKAWA CORPORATION, Tokyo.
English translation rights arranged with KADOKAWA CORPORATION, Tokyo, through TUTTLE-MORI AGENCY, INC., Tokyo.

English translation © 2020 by Yen Press, LLC

Yen On
150 West 30th Street, 19th Floor
New York, NY 10001

Visit us at yenpress.com
facebook.com/yenpress
twitter.com/yenpress
yenpress.tumblr.com
instagram.com/yenpress

First Yen On Edition: September 2020

Yen On is an imprint of Yen Press, LLC.
The Yen On name and logo are trademarks of Yen Press, LLC.

The publisher is not responsible for websites (or their content) that are not owned by the publisher.

Library of Congress Cataloging-in-Publication Data
Names: Akatsuki, Natsume, author. | Mishima, Kurone, 1991– illustrator. | Wetnight, Alex, translator.
Title: Konosuba, an explosion on this wonderful world! bonus story / Natsume Akatsuki ; illustration by Kurone Mishima ; translation by Alex Wetnight ; cover art by Kurone Mishima.
Other titles: Kono subarashii sekai ni shukufuku wo! supin ofu zoku. English
Description: First Yen On edition. | New York, NY : Yen On, 2020.
Identifiers: LCCN 2020026844 | ISBN 9781975387068 (v. 1 ; trade paperback)
Subjects: CYAC: Fantasy. | Magic—Fiction.
Classification: LCC PZ7.1.A38 Ko 2020 | DDC [Fic]—dc23
LC record available at https://lccn.loc.gov/2020026844

ISBNs: 978-1-9753-8706-8 (paperback)
978-1-9753-8707-5 (ebook)

10 9 8 7 6 5 4 3 2 1

LSC-C

Printed in the United States of America

Prologue

It was the night of the fireworks show I attended with a special someone. Unable to fulfill my promise to that certain person, I was trudging home, a bit disheartened.

Some suspicious-looking people had approached the mansion of a detestable noble named Undyne and were observing the building from a distance.

My heart started beating out of my chest at the sight of their familiar masks. *Strange, was I always so excitable?* I'd meant to be more well behaved and levelheaded than that...

Making up my mind, I called to the two of them.

"E-excuse me... Aren't you two the Silver-Haired Thief Brigade?"

Before I knew it, I was introducing myself to them. The two shook with surprise at the sound of my voice coming from behind them.

I decided to ask them something I'd been wondering for a long time.

"When you snuck into the royal palace, was it to protect the princess because of the dangerous magical items in her possession?"

They answered my question, saying, "Indeed we did. We're what they call 'chivalrous thieves.' Usually, we're friends of the common man, but we can't look the other way when a helpless girl is in danger, even if she's a princess. When someone's in trouble, we'll sneak into any place, whether it's a nobleman's mansion or the royal palace. That's how the Masked Thief Brigade rolls."

The details might've been off, but his statement was clear.

"Your name is Megumin, right? Actually, we're looking for a certain something that lies in this manor—something necessary to the future of mankind. While it's true that stealing is not a deed to be praised, for us, this is something we need to do, even with a bounty on our heads."

The eyes under that mask held a firm determination. Somehow, looking into them gave me a familiar feeling.

Not breaking my gaze, I continued to listen.

"We're going into the mansion to steal—to acquire a trump card against the Demon King's army. If you say you're going to snitch on us, we won't stop you...but believe me, this is for the sake of all humanity."

Basically, these two, even with large bounties on their heads, were going to continue their work, regardless of whether the army of the Demon King—or even the whole world—was against them. They didn't care if that was all they were doing or that they would have their work cut out for them.

The two thieves talked excitedly between themselves, like two partners who'd long been at each other's side. For some reason, seeing them chat gave me a wrenching feeling in my chest.

Saying good-bye, I longingly looked back again and again. Finally, I pretended to leave.

It was on that day...

...I resolved to help those two from the shadows as they continued to fight all on their own...

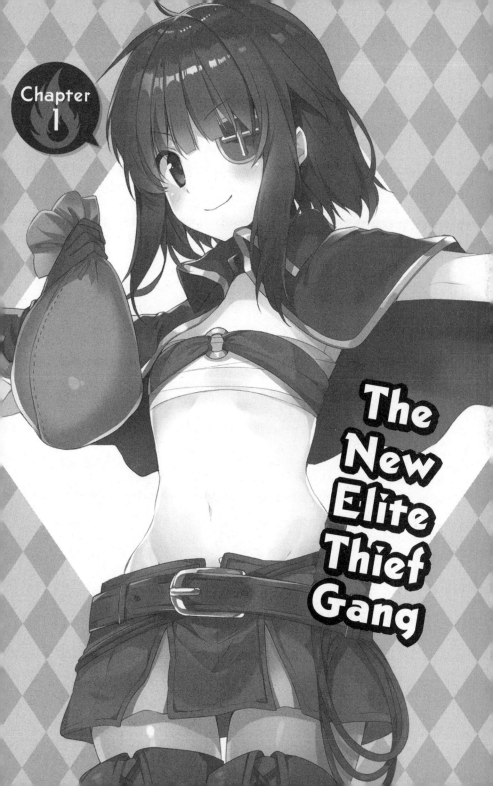

Chapter 1

The New Elite Thief Gang

1

There was a town called Axel.

It was a town where fledgling adventurers gathered to seek companions, and it was also a place famous for being very safe.

I was at Axel's Adventurers Guild when...

"St-stoppp! What are you doing?!"

Some completely undeserved abuse was being hurled at me.

The Guild's receptionist lady was holding the paper I'd posted on the bulletin board as she spoke to me.

"What do you mean, 'What are you doing?!' This bulletin board is for adventurers to recruit party members. If you're looking for playmates, go somewhere else!"

"Playmates? How rude! This is a legitimate search for the most stalwart of companions—if you have a complaint about where I stuck the flyer, let's hear it!"

Demanding the return of my recruitment listing, I went off on the beautiful, well-endowed receptionist lady who was thrusting her breasts toward me quite ostentatiously.

"The fact that you aren't just playing makes it all the worse! I'm not complaining about where you put it! I'm complaining about the kind of people you're recruiting!"

Holding the piece of paper in front of me, she read aloud the words written on it.

"'Seeking Thieves. Only enthusiastic individuals unafraid to commit crimes to do what's right. Main duties include assaulting residences of nobles...'"

The nearby adventurers, who'd been listening, looked at me like I was a pitiful child.

"...Fine. Truthfully, I wanted to limit it to Thief classes, but other classes can join, too. I'll rewrite it."

"That's not the issue! I'm asking you not to use the Guild's bulletin board to recruit accomplices to crimes!"

...It was back during the time of the Eris Appreciation Festival when I ran into the thief gang I had become so enamored with.

There was the silver-haired leader, whose mouth was hidden behind their mask. With the leader was a mysterious man wearing a cool-looking domino of his own. Such an awesome disguise meant there was no way he was just some ordinary person.

The silver-haired one, the boss, seemed pretty lively, I guess. They gave off the impression of being a trustworthy companion.

What stuck with me was the other robber who hid his face. He wore a replica of Vanir's mask. The guy looked really familiar. There was something about him that put me at ease, even though I had most definitely never met him before.

Plus, he rolled with a bandit crew. He was a chivalrous thief and wore a mask.

...I was in love.

To bear so many traits that tugged at my heartstrings, this could not have been some common man.

Truthfully, I wanted them to let me into their crew. Unfortunately, I didn't have any thieving skills.

"...And so, as a fan of theirs, I thought I would take it upon myself to make a subgroup and recruit people to assist in their righteous endeavors."

"If you form such a dumb party, I'll put a bounty on you."

With the receptionist lady having confiscated my flyer, I surveyed the Guild Hall's interior.

If she wasn't going to allow my recruitment posting, then I had no choice but to scout members myself. But the adventurers who'd been listening to our exchange wouldn't look me in the eye.

I approached a young guy nearby who looked like a Thief. I smiled as hard as I could to put him at ease.

"You look bored, sir. Could I ask you something?"

"Sorry, I'm busy counting the wood grains in the table. Ask me later."

I found myself grabbing on to him when he started making a show of counting the little flecks.

"You were looking bored just a second ago. What is your problem?!"

"Give me a break; don't involve me in this! Why me, of all people, when you've got that guy you can use all you like?! He has Thief skills, doesn't he?!"

"Of course. He was the first one I asked. But he said he would come play when it was less hot outside. It seems he does not think I am serious about making a group to support the thief gang."

"Obviously. Anyone would think you were joking if you said you wanted to support crooks with bounties on their heads."

I pounded the table with a *bam* as he nodded at his own statement.

"That heroic bunch is working day and night to save the future of mankind, even when others continue to bad-mouth them! It looks like I need to tell you all about that part first!"

"Stop it—I don't wanna hear about that, and I don't want anything to do with you! Here, I'll give you some peanuts to snack on, so go bother someone else!"

...I do not understand.

To think I would have to clear up society's misunderstandings

10   Konosuba: An Explosion on This Wonderful World! Bonus Story

about them before I could even start to help those whom I admired so much…

With a bowl of nuts in one hand, I munched idly as I surveyed my surroundings…

Naturally, though everyone was averting their eyes, I sensed a look from behind me.

When I fixed my eyes upon them, the person whose gaze met mine looked down in a panic, only to later glance up at me, as if in expectation.

…

"Miss Looks-Like-a-Thief there, could I ask you something?"

"Hey, Megumin, didn't we just lock eyes?!"

As I called to a different young woman nearby, the look-away-glance-up-girl, also known as Yunyun, kicked her chair over and stood.

"It's so annoying when you stare like you want my attention even though you don't come over and talk to me yourself! If you have something to say, just say it!"

"Stop it! All right, I will, so stop pulling my hair!"

As I grabbed at the ever-troublesome Yunyun, she twisted her face into a resolute expression.

"I don't know what you're gonna do—I just thought I'd like to be a part of it…," she said with unusual initiative. Actually, there had been rumors this girl was involved with some strange folks recently.

Perhaps her involvement with those weird people had made this girl a little more assertive.

However…

"What are you talking about? You are already the subleader of my crew, you know. Your name is even on the list."

"What? I never heard anything about that! Wait, that's what you're doing? Inviting people to join some shady group?!"

I found myself lashing out at Yunyun as she raised her voice in surprise.

"What do you mean, 'shady group'?! It is a pure, just, and respectable thief gang who steals for the sake of the world and its people!"

"That makes no sense! I've got an awful feeling about this, so count me out!"

As I was arguing with Yunyun, the woman I'd been trying to talk to left the Guild in a panic.

I grabbed Yunyun by the hand as she attempted to flee, too.

"You are a member of the Crimson Magic Clan—what are you afraid of?! I swear, everyone is on guard because of our spat just now. Look, do not stay there pouting; we are going into town to find some members! New members will also be your companions. Get it? You can make some friends."

"If you think I'll do whatever you ask just because of the promise of new friends, you're dead wroooong!"

2

"...Look, what about him? He looks like he would make a good bandit."

"*Shh*, Megumin, you're too loud! He's just a regular person who happens to look scary; he's not an adventurer! Maybe that girl over there instead. She seems about our age…"

"She's even more of a normie. You know we are looking for thieves, not friends, right?"

We were on Axel's main street.

Yunyun, who'd come along despite her griping, sat with me on a bench along the road. Together, we observed the people going here and there.

Yes, this was so when we saw any talent who made us think *This is the one!* we could immediately recruit them.

Right from the get-go, however, Yunyun's opinions and mine were so different that we hadn't been able to talk to anyone.

"Ah, what about that girl? I can't see her face under the hood of her robe, but she looks around our age. That sword she's wearing means she's not just a regular person, right?"

As she spoke, Yunyun pointed at a petite young woman wearing a drab mantle. I couldn't see her hair color, but the eyes peering out from her hood were a clear and bright shade of blue…

"Wait a second. Why is that girl here in town?"

"Wh-what's wrong, Megumin? Do you know her?"

We watched; the hooded girl wobbled as she walked, then looked anxiously here and there, like she was highly interested in what was around her.

Just then, a middle-aged man running a kebab stall called out to her.

"You there, young lady, how about a freshly grilled kebab? I'll lower the price for a cutie like you, okay? Just one million eris each if you buy now."

"Kebabs… I've never seen food like this before. One million eris each? Well then, could I get three?" Having taken the man's joke seriously, the young girl in the hood took out her wallet from an inner pocket…

"What are you doing?! You must not take out so much money in a place like this!"

"Huh?! Ahhh! It's Megumin!"

I ran up to the young girl—who I knew to be Princess Iris—as she took a high-value coin from her wallet like it was nothing. I snatched the money she was about to offer to the vendor.

Not hesitating, I began lecturing Iris, ignoring the kebab man, who was frozen in place at the sight of such a valuable coin.

"He was joking about the one million; he actually means one hundred eris each. In what world do they sell kebabs at a price that high?"

"R-really? I don't know anything about market prices…"

Just then, the previously frozen vendor held out a skewer with a serious expression.

"No, no, one million eris each is correct. You're a pretty young girl, so I'll give you a deal—one million for three."

"Is it okay to take them for such a low price? Thank you so much!"

"Do not be deceived! This man is trying to rip you off now that he knows you're inexperienced! Here, three hundred eris! If you want to cheat an ignorant girl, then you will have to go through me first!!"

…With Iris and her fairly priced kebabs in tow, the three of us relocated to a nearby park.

"I swear, why are you wandering around a place like this by yourself? What is your bodyguard doing?" I asked Iris again as she wasted no time bringing one of her just-purchased skewers to her mouth.

The princess relaxed into a happy smile. This was, perhaps, her first experience with this kind of commoner food.

"What do you mean, 'bodyguard'? My name is Illis. Maybe you have me confused with someone else? …Still, these 'kebab' things are delicious. This might be the first time I've eaten something so warm. You can have one if you like."

Feigning ignorance, she offered Yunyun and me one each. Apparently, she wanted us to use this "Illis" alias.

I took one of the skewers.

"*Sigh…* Well, what are you doing in a place like this, Lady Illis? This town is one of the safer ones, but you never know what kind of mistakes might happen, you know?"

"Stop it with 'Lady Illis.' Just call me Illis… Hee-hee, actually, I came to this town in secret the other day for some fun. I wasn't able to see Kazuma, but I met an interesting individual… It made me realize that this world is still full of oddballs, so I've snuck away like this to learn more about society."

At her sudden and shocking utterance, I spat out a bit of the kebab I was munching on. The imperial capital must've been in an awful uproar by now.

"Here, here, you have one, too."

"Ah, thanks, Illis! Ummm, my name is Yunyun… Hey, Megumin. This girl has blond hair and blue eyes. Is she a noble?" Yunyun asked as she took a skewer from Iris, bringing it timidly to her mouth.

"No, I'm Illis, a granddaughter of Chirimendonya in the capital. I am no noble girl."

Who in the world could've influenced her to say such a strange thing?

And what was Chirimendonya supposed to be?

"She's insisting on it, so just humor her… We have a problem, however—now that we have happened upon Illis, we cannot simply leave her alone…"

We couldn't encounter a princess only to leave her by herself. Seeing me in doubt, Iris, kebab in hand, cocked her head to the side.

"What were the two of you doing here?"

For a moment, I wondered if answering Iris's innocent question truthfully was the best idea. However, I was certain this pure maiden didn't harbor any ill feelings toward the noble pilferers I admired.

"Actually, we are hoping to create a subgroup to the Silver-Haired Thief Brigade."

"What's that?! Tell me all about it!"

Wait, I didn't expect her to be this enthusiastic.

"Basically, just unofficially calling ourselves their subgroup, unofficially recruiting companions, and unofficially supporting their crew. That is what we are going for."

"Sounds fun! Might there be some kind of test for getting into this group?"

With Iris again showing a positive reaction, I shook my head to make her rethink this.

"What, you want to join? That will not do; this is not for play. There is much to be done, like constructing a secret base to be our hideout and expanding our forces. So of course we would need to have our members do their share of the work, too."

"A secret base!"

For some reason, Iris's eyes brightened at my attempt to dissuade her.

"U-ummm… In addition, we expect to be using illegal means to punish crooked nobles…"

"'Punish crooked nobles'!"

For some reason, Iris's eyes brightened even more at my attempt to dissuade her.

"By all means, let me in! Let me join the two of you!"

Seeing Iris flushed and clenching her fists, as if something had pulled at her heartstrings, even Yunyun was forgiving about bringing Iris along. "Hey, Megumin, if she's this enthusiastic, surely we can let her in? …N-not that I'm happy to have a kid my age as a companion or anything."

I wondered if we wouldn't be hung the day word got out that we let the princess join such a dangerous group.

Actually, the people who put the bounty on my beloved Silver-Haired Thief Brigade in the first place were close to this girl.

"W-well, when you put it that way, I think it's fine. However, as this is no game for us, either, I shall have you take the entrance exam. If I judge you to be deserving of admittance, in addition to having good marks, I shall bestow upon you the position of left hand to the gang leader."

"Hey, Megumin, just asking, but who's the right hand? I'm just letting you put my name on the roster for numbers, you know? Don't go making me part of the top brass without my permission, all right?!"

Taking no notice of Yunyun and her cold feet, Iris's face was sparkling.

3

…We stood on a familiar plain just outside of town.

"A-are you okay, Illis?! That is a much bigger frog than we usually see around here!"

We were trying to measure the girl's abilities against Axel's famous monster and our sworn enemy, the frog.

"It's fine! The royal family… I mean, the Chirimendonya clan is strong!"

Was Chirimendonya the name of a clan like the Crimson Magic Clan?

Iris drew the sword at her waist and took a combat stance against her fearsome opponent.

"*Exterion!*"

She swung with a shout, even though the frog was still quite a distance away.

Her enormous and lavishly decorated sword, a weapon that didn't match her petite frame in the slightest, gently cut through the air despite its large size, and...

...the frog, which had been leaping toward us, abruptly fell to the ground in two halves.

""Wha—?!"" Yunyun and I blurted out. Iris sheathed her sword in satisfaction as we watched.

"What do you think, Megumin? Do I pass the test?"

"Huh?! ...Ummm, this is still the first stage! The creature you defeated is a monster any adventurer with decent equipment can hunt! It is only natural for you to beat it in one hit, you see!"

"You know you got eaten by one of those frogs..."

Ignoring a voice from behind me, I decided to assign Iris an additional test...

"...*Exterion!*"

"Hold on now—what is that attack you keep using?! Do you not find it a bit overpowered?! How are the mighty One-Punch Bears the ones getting one-shot?!"

Iris's power seemed to have no limit, so I'd kept raising the difficulty level of the monsters for her to put down.

"This is an attack only usable by those deemed worthy by the holy sword, which has been passed down in my clan for generations. It's a special ability that can unleash a fierce slashing blow!"

"Might that be what the hero was said to possess? The legendary—? N-no, let us not think too deeply about this."

The royal family was known for having had a powerful hero marry into their lineage, incorporating that mighty warrior's strengths into the royal bloodline. Thus, a great training foundation was passed down to members of the ruling family, most of whom were already unfairly strong…

"In any case, it is the weapon that is strong, right? My thief gang will get into some rough work, so we cannot let people in if they, themselves, are not up to snuff. What I want to see is your real power. Please show me that, at least."

"Hey, Megumin, isn't Illis pretty obviously stronger than we are? Why don't you just admit it?" Yunyun said as she tugged on my clothes. However, if I simply admitted that now, I'd be dishonored.

"All right, I'll go defeat that gaggle of monsters over there without using my holy sword." Iris pointed her finger at a group visible in the distance while Yunyun and I whispered to each other…

"Er, isn't that a gaggle of goblins?! You must beware—monster types as tempting as that usually have a formidable Beginner's Bane nearby…!"

Even as I gave the warning, the princess was already stretching out her hand toward the group of creatures…!

"Sacred Lightning Blare—!"

At the same time Iris shouted, a blinding light flashed from within the middle of the goblin pack, unleashing streaks of white lightning that mowed them down as a violent gust blew forth…!

4

Arriving back in Axel, I clapped my hands together.

"Okay, the first stage of testing is now over. I will admit you have *somewhat* decent-enough skill for a newcomer. Though, since we are a thief gang, we do not have much need for combat prowess. So power alone does not put you in our good graces."

"Come on, Megumin! That's completely different from what you said before! What happened to 'not letting people in who aren't up to snuff because we'll be performing rough work'?"

Yunyun, who'd been somewhat in awe of Iris's power, came back to her senses and scolded me.

"P-pipe down. She passed the first test without issue, so what's the problem?!"

"You're saying 'first test,' but there wasn't anything like that for me, was there?! Anyway, this girl is obviously more powerful than—"

"S-stop it! You mustn't say any more; once you admit defeat, it's all over!"

To be honest, I'd underestimated the strength of the royal family. The power of the royal family and others of nobility was well-known, but I never would've thought it would be like this.

Actually, maybe this girl should've been the one to go up against the Demon King.

"But to also take out the Beginner's Bane lying in wait at the same time, Illis really can use some incredible magic. Actually, even as a Crimson Magic Clanner, I've never heard of that spell before…"

"It's one of the spells passed down through generations in the royal family…I mean, the Chirimendonya clan. The magic emits lightning that conceals a sacred power. Apparently, it's an original spell said to have been the legendary hero's specialty."

The mystery surrounding the Chirimendonya family only kept getting deeper.

"So what sort of test is the second one? I have confidence in my physical abilities, so I'll take on any trial!"

Seeing Iris so full of enthusiasm, I held my head, wondering what to do.

I could imagine what an uproar there'd be if it got out that I had let the princess into my thief gang without anyone's permission. To be honest, I'd meant to find some kind of fault to make her give up on joining, but…

Just then, Yunyun suddenly offered an idea. "There's no point in testing her strength anymore. Maybe an intelligence or street-smarts test would be better? Of course, Illis seems to have a good upbringing, so she's probably academically gifted as well."

"That's it!"

I nodded enthusiastically at Yunyun's casually uttered words.

This applicant was a princess who'd had a gifted education. Thus, an academic test would be meaningless. Street smarts, however…

"What is necessary for thieves is not power in battle. And a high IQ is good and all, but the most important thing is common sense! I shall test you, Illis, to measure how streetwise you are!"

"Megumin, as someone so exceptionally lacking in such a thing herself—even in Axel—it's a joke for you to measure someone else's— Ow, ow!"

As I was pulling Yunyun's hair for her unnecessary interruption, Iris, who was somewhat hesitant, clenched her fists nevertheless.

"N-no problem! Even I, having slipped away to explore the town like this, should have some decent street smarts by now! Don't hold back—begin this test!"

…To make a long story short, it went terribly.

"Miss, that is not something you eat as is. You peel off the skin first and eat the inside."

When I had her shop around on the commercial strip, Iris stopped to bite into a freshly purchased mango as if it was her first time seeing unpeeled fruit.

The blond girl blushed, embarrassed at the shop owner's admonishment. Then she looked at me helplessly.

I swear, this ignorant princess is so hopeless…

"I cannot say I am surprised—after all, up until now, you have never eaten fruit unless it was peeled and served on a plate, right? I shall teach you what everyone here knows. When it comes to fruit, first you remove the skin. After eating the inner flesh, fry up the seeds for a snack. Later, you can boil and eat the peeled skin."

"You're off, too, Megumin! Normally you just throw away the skin and seeds!"

For a moment, my beliefs seemed about ready to crumble under Yunyun's unexpected criticism.

"Th-that cannot be. The seeds are just as delicious as sunflower seeds when you fry them until they're nice and dry; and if you boil it slowly, the skin is edible, too! You were the biggest oddball in Crimson Magic Village, you know, Yunyun. I swear, kids these days, no common sense…"

"Hold on a second, you! I'm pretty sure I'm the most sensible one out of all three of us, you know?! Speaking of, Illis, you can't bite into that until you've paid for it!"

"S-sorry! Someone in my entourage always went ahead and paid for me…!"

An unexpected weakness of mine had been exposed, and I couldn't afford to continue the trial like this.

Hmm, Iris certainly is outstanding both in battle and in talent, but…

"Hey, Megumin, I don't know what you're hesitating for, but why don't you just let Illis join already? Not getting to be a part of things can hurt someone's feelings…"

"That is seriously depressing coming from you, so please stop! Fine, we will set aside this test. For now, we will call this a temporary provisional induction. We do not know what your attendants will say if they find out, after all."

Iris's face lit up as I gave in to Yunyun.

"Your temp status means that you are a grunt. You will have to do what I say as leader, okay?"

Hearing that, Yunyun seemed to remember something.

"Speaking of, why are you suddenly the one in charge? Not that I want to be leader, but as your rival, I don't like you going and making me your underling like I lost."

"Look at this girl being a pain again. Is it not obvious that I am the strongest and most dependable adult among us? As such, I have to be the one to lead."

My two minions, seemingly unconvinced at my reasoning, both looked uneasy.

"The royal fa… The Chirimendonya clan is strong. Would you like to try fighting me?"

"Battle…might be difficult, but I'm the most mature among us, am I not? I have common sense, and I'm the tallest, to boot."

Good grief, I thought, shaking my head at the tiresome things my two underlings had said.

"Getting worked up so easily like that sure is childish. Besides, obviously I am the most adultlike, don't you think? After all…"

A little while later.

"I have asked a certain guy if he would like to come hang out in my room tonight, so."

I revealed the promise I'd made with a special someone just the other day.

""Whaaaaaaa—?!""

"Wai—! Wh-what are you doing—stoppit! Stop iiit! Please let me go; I shall have you stop pulling on my robe!"

"Come on, Megumin, what do you mean?! That 'certain guy' is Kazuma, right?! D-do you mean to cross the line with him?!"

"Ohhh, did you invite him to your room?! He'd probably jump on any invite he received. That is improper for a lady like you, Megumin. As his little sister, I cannot overlook such a debauched relationship!"

The two girls had grabbed me. Pushing them away, I fixed my collar.

"I am old enough to be married already. Anyway, we are a young man and woman living together under one roof, so surely there is nothing wrong with it at this point?"

Hearing my carefree words and understanding the obvious difference in my status, the two of them were pale and shaken.

"Well then, do you have any objections to my being leader?"

5

Having demonstrated my overwhelming superiority, I led my minions our original destination…

"I am begging you. Can you please do something?"

"Impossible." The landlord's answer was immediate and cold.

"What in the world are you unhappy with?! You mean to say you cannot trust me, who came to repel the Demon King's many generals?! No other wizard is so deserving of deferred payment as I am!"

"I'm telling you that it can't be done, no matter what you say! You have no collateral, nor do you have the funds. Yet, you're cheeky enough to ask to rent the largest building in town?! And while your party has had some success, you should realize that it's also been selected as the group most likely to get wiped out!"

"Wh-what?! Who could have made such an unfair evaluation?!"

Having come to a landlord in Axel, we were in discussions to acquire a hideout. As you can see, however, we were being treated very unfairly.

"In any case, thirty thousand eris is not enough for a security deposit. I have done this job for a long time, but this is the first time anyone has asked me to fork over the best building in town for such a price."

"*Ugh...* I guess I have no choice. This was my nest egg for emergencies, but...," I said, adding onto the table my reserve of ten thousand eris, which the landlord flicked away with his index finger.

"Hey, what are you doing to my savings?! I saved up very carefully for that!"

"Upping thirty thousand eris to forty won't change a thing! Please leave already!"

Just then, as I was having it out with the landlord, there was a tug on my mantle from behind.

"Hey, Megumin, don't you think you're being a bit unreasonable? I guess you were serious about creating a hideout or whatever. I'm all for the idea of having a place for all our friends to get together and relax, so let's head back for today and think of how we can come up with the money."

I gnashed my teeth at Yunyun's words, thinking about what to do. But then...

"Excuse me... How much would it cost to rent the largest building in town?" Iris timidly asked the landlord, poking just her head out from behind us.

"The biggest in this town would cost, ohhh, two million eris a month. Adding in the security deposit and such, I suppose it'd run around five million."

Five million…

I gently pushed Yunyun toward the landlord.

"…I will throw in the right to have this girl call you 'sir' every day, so can't you lower the price just a little?"

"Why do I have to do that?!"

I took a defensive stance against Yunyun's strangling attempt; then Iris tapped me on the back.

"What is it, Illis? These are important negotiations here, so please stay out of the…," I started. Then a gasp escaped me.

"Um, would this be enough money?"

Iris held out an incredibly high-value eris bill.

Even the landlord was frozen at the sight. Yunyun's face went stiff.

"Th-that certainly would be enough money, but to lease the building, I would need a trustworthy guarantor who can vouch for you…," the man said apologetically. Iris looked troubled.

"Um, is this good enough?" she asked, taking a pendant out from between her breasts, and…

"My sincerest apologies! For you, I will lease any number of buildings! No charge, of course! I will bring the key at once, so please do wait right there!"

At the sight of the trinket, the landlord flew off in a panic to the back of the shop.

Watching him go, Yunyun said with a nervous look, "…Hey, Illis, are you from a really prestigious family, by chance?"

"…She is nothing more than a lowly grunt in our crew of bandits."

"Yes, I'm a grunt!"

Yunyun was taken aback at seeing the blond girl so happy being called such a demeaning thing. "But you must be of high birth to have changed that man's attitude, right? …Hey, Megumin, is it okay to involve Illis in these dumb games? Are we doing something incredibly stupid?"

Her mouth twitching, my self-proclaimed rival only now seemed to have realized the seriousness of things, but it was too late.

"Sorry to keep you waiting; here is the key! ...I do look forward to your continued business with our realty office in the future, if you please."

With the same fervor as when he left the room, the landlord flashed a stiff smile. With key in hand, sweat ran down his face.

"...Hey, Megumin. If I cause any more trouble to the police, I don't think I'll be able to look the other villagers in the eye..."

"It's fine; if anyone asks, we've been guarding Illis from danger. Nothing more, nothing less. Understand?"

6

There stood a large, splendid mansion in the first-class district near the center of Axel.

Starting today, this building, which made my own mansion look like a regular house, would be our hideout.

As Yunyun and I looked up at the enormous abode, we exchanged some muttered words.

"...We need to decide on the name of our thief gang soon. Also, let us make this place the Axel branch."

"Hey, Megumin, exactly how big a group are you planning to make? I thought it was just going to be for pretend at first, but I'm a bit scared at how out of control things are getting."

I hadn't expected things to go smoothly, either, so I was actually pretty flustered, but I couldn't let them know that.

Never would I have expected to get the best mansion in town on the day our band of crooks was formed.

"What a big mansion! It might even be larger than my father's summer home!"

Ignoring Iris and her singularly out-of-place impression of the building, I opened the front door.

Perhaps all nobles' homes were designed in a similar fashion, as past the entrance was a great hall, just like my own.

Although the landlord had cared for the interior well enough, there still wasn't much in the way of furniture, with nothing more than a big sofa and table.

Throwing my body upon the cushioned seat, I made a declaration as I lazed about.

"Starting today, this is our secret base. Henceforth, everyone shall come here when we scheme, or discuss plans of action, or when we are bored and feel like it. I guess you could call it our hangout. You will each need to hold on to your own key."

At the word *hangout*, Yunyun's eyes glowed red, showing her delight. Iris, whatever she was happy about, leaped impolitely onto the sofa with a huge smile on her face.

Before long, Yunyun joined us, sitting on the edge with a relaxed grin. I sat myself up straight to address my underlings.

"The hideout fell into our hands with unexpected ease, but connections and family power are also a kind of talent. Let us use what we can without reservation… Now, then." I placed my hands on the table. "Okay, let us discuss our plan of action."

With those introductory remarks, it was here that I finally began my explanation to them…

"…Now you understand. They are not lining their own pockets. Despite acting as chivalrous thieves, friends of the common man, they are being chased as criminals with large bounties on their heads. Nevertheless, they continue on for the sake of the world, for the sake of mankind! Even if no one knows of their actions or understands them, their struggle continues, even now!"

"Amazing…! What brave and true people…! Megumin, I've made up my mind! Up till just now, I was reluctantly going along with what I thought was another silly game you started, but from now on, I'm serious about helping!"

The part about "another silly game you started" gave me pause, but she was on board now, so whatever.

Iris, however, had been quiet for a while at this point. When I looked over at her, she was trembling.

"I—I…"

"Illis? What on earth is the matter? Your face is red and your eyes watery…"

Seeming to have not heard what I'd said, Iris struck the table with a *bam* and stood up.

"I'm going to my father right now to whine until he removes the bounty on that thief gang! If that doesn't work, then I'll just go to Kazuma and dote on him!"

"What is this girl saying all of a sudden?! Forget the bounty and whatnot—surely there is no need to dote on Kazuma!"

With the way the conversation had been going, why in the world would she go and say something like that?

"We can't look the other way when a helpless girl is in danger, even if she's a princess. When someone's in trouble, we'll sneak into any place, whether it's a nobleman's mansion or the royal palace. That's how the Masked Thief Brigade rolls."

Yes, all I had done was teach her those words the masked man had said when I first encountered those awesome thieves.

"Anyway, this is our objective moving forward. We are still only three people. With all of us being so young, even if we try to extend our territory and expand our forces, surely no one will take us seriously. Therefore, we must raise our fame gradually, gathering more intimidating and competent members. That way we can eventually stand shoulder to shoulder with the Silver-Haired Thief Brigade!"

Having heard my impassioned speech, both my minions were likely considering who would be suitable as a member.

"'Intimidating and competent members'… The people I'm thinking of have the perfect image for being bandits or outlaws, but absolutely nothing good will come of that…"

While Yunyun pondered and muttered quietly, Iris crossed her arms, looking troubled.

"Er, Megumin. When I came to this town before, there was quite an outstanding individual who did a lot for me. Shall we invite them?"

"An 'outstanding individual,' you say? I'm not sure what led to you meeting someone in this town, but what kind of person were they?"

Iris cocked her head slightly at my question.

"Their name was Hachibee, a cheery individual who spent most of the day laughing. They loved flattery and thoroughly complimented and doted on me. They said they would help out with anything for the right price."

"Listen, Illis, you need to cut ties with them right away! What I am seeking is someone who can sing and dance and fight—someone hilarious and extraordinary!"

Well, we'd only just formed our righteous criminal group. It was pretty outrageous to expect more members right off the bat.

We needed to take our time from now on to increase our membership.

In order to put our original plan into action, I said, "For now, have a look at this, you two. Let us discuss tonight's plan." I spread out a map of the town on the table...

7

Our target was a certain nobleman's second home.

We watched as some soldiers guarded the front gate.

"...Hey, Megumin. I was wondering this before, but are you an imbecile? How in the world did you get the best grades in the village?"

Ignoring Yunyun, who'd been saying things like that for a while, I got back to observing the mansion.

"The number of guards and the scale of the building... If I wanted, it would only need one hit with Explosion."

"Hey, Megumin, you ought to take the title of the Crimson Magic Clan's number one idiot!"

We couldn't afford drawing the attention of the people in the manor, so I covered Yunyun's loud mouth to silence her. Iris tugged the edge of my cape, looking uncertain.

"Excuse me, Megumin…? I may not have much worldly wisdom, but even I can tell this is a bad idea. Why don't we at least find some kind of evidence first…?"

I smiled confidently to reassure her.

"It will be fine, Illis. The Crimson Magic Clan is skilled in crafting magic items, and its members have this saying: 'Make what you don't have.'"

"Wait a second! That's not what that means!"

Despite Yunyun's reflexive criticism, I kept my eyes fixed on the target. "It's fine, Yunyun; we have Illis. With her at our backs, we can never lose in court."

"You know, I was trying not to ask this, but I have to! Just who are you, Illis?! Is this perhaps something we shouldn't be doing right now?!"

My self-proclaimed rival was shouting something, but I just stared at the space above the manor, looking where best to center my spell. Then suddenly…!

"Lady Ir…! L-Lady Illis, I finally found you!"

From behind us, there came a voice on the verge of tears. Turning to look, we saw a woman dressed up in a white suit and wearing a sword at her hip. I could tell from the tears welling in the corners of her eyes and her shortness of breath that she must have been searching desperately for the princess.

As I recalled, her name was Claire, or something like that. Anyway, that lady was serving as Iris's bodyguard.

"Claire?! H-how did you know I was in town?!"

Iris stepped back, looking stunned, like she hadn't expected to be found.

"Do you know how long I have been serving you, Lady Illis? As a loyal attendant, I make note of every detail about you: how much you grew in a week, how many times you yawned in a day, and how many

times you tried to put your green peppers off to the side at mealtime. Naturally, I know all about what you have been up to!"

Ah, I get it now. This person is a weirdo.

"C-Claire, you're weirding me out! Still, I can't believe you'd find me so easily… Anyway, I have something to ask! Can I stay at Kazuma's mansion? Just for tonight?"

"No."

Snatching Iris by the shoulders, as if to say *That's the one thing I can't agree to*, the attendant hugged the princess tightly, not allowing her to escape.

"Let me go, Claire! If I don't go tonight, he might get seduced!"

"That's great! A man like that deserves to be seduced, even henpecked! Now, Lady Illis, you will see what happens if you continue to whine!" the woman in the white suit shouted as she tightened her grip on the princess.

"C-Claire? I can't talk like this, so can you please ease up for now?"

Ignoring her plea, Claire rubbed the tip of her nose on Iris's hair and inhaled happily.

"No. This is your punishment, Lady Illis. To make sure nothing like this happens again, I shall harden my heart, hugging and drawing you clo— Ow, ow! W-wait a second, please, Lady Illis! I'm sorry! I apologize for taking it too far, so please stop squeezing me so hard!"

The blond girl retaliated by hugging back with all her might. Claire, whose body was making the sorts of noises it never should, freed herself and looked my way.

"Long time no see, Miss Megumin. I am indebted to you for protecting Lady Illis. However, I will set up surveillance on the capital's transport shop hereafter. As such, I am sure Lady Illis will be unable to come to town again. So please say your good-byes now…"

Iris looked down at the ground, dejected and deflated.

Judging by how upset Claire was, Iris really must've slipped away from the palace without permission this time.

Palace security would probably tighten from now on, and with her unable to use the teleporter, our difference in status would mean we'd probably never see each other again.

With a gentle nudge from Claire, Iris stood in front of me, looking like a kid who wanted to keep playing.

In a voice only my underling—in her sudden kowtowing defeatism—would hear, I whispered, "Keep your ears open after you get back to the palace. I will send you a signal. Starting tomorrow, when you hear that sound, please come to the front gate of the capital, however you can."

It was just like we were making a promise to play together again.

"Huh?"

Lifting her head, the blond girl stared blankly, not seeming to understand what I'd said.

"You may be a temp, but you are still a member of our thieving crew. Once you have joined, do not think you can leave so easily."

Hearing that, Iris's face lit up.

"Yes, of course, boss!" she said with a huge smile.

"…Lady Illis, I don't know what you're whispering about, but I'm not letting you get out anymore, understand? I-it won't do you any good to look up at me with a cute face like that! Come on—let's go to the transport shop. Lain is likely to be in tears by now, looking for you in the capital."

Iris gave it her best, making all kinds of pleas, but Claire still took her away to the transport shop.

"She's gone…," Yunyun whispered.

"Yunyun. You learned Teleport, did you not?"

At this, my self-proclaimed rival cocked her head slightly.

"Huh? Ahhh, yeah. I finally learned it recently so that I could go home to Crimson Magic Village whenever, but…"

"I see. Then I have a request for you. Let us go to the transport shop now. Then, after they send us to the capital, could you register that as one of your destinations?"

"The capital? …I mean, that's fine, but you aren't plotting anything weird, are you?"

Plotting? How outrageous.

I was merely making sure we could meet with our grunt whenever we needed to.

"Calling it 'plotting' is so rude. I am simply going to take a little trip to finish some errands. It is too bad about today, but our plans will have to be postponed. All right, let's go!"

"I don't mind, but what's that look in your eye, Megumin?! I've got a bad feeling about this!"

...After teleporting to the capital from the transport shop, we went straight to the exterior of the front gate.

"Okay, please register this area as a teleportation destination. I have something I need to do right now, so once you are finished, please come find me."

"I guess that's okay, but what's this thing you need to do? Does it have something to do with whatever you were whispering to Illis earlier?"

Yunyun looked a bit anxious, but I just turned my back. I walked toward a hillock far from the gate.

Yep, at this distance, the people of the capital shouldn't be able to see me.

I psyched myself up and began to chant a spell for the sake of my minion...

"Hold on! Megumin, what are you doing?! You don't mean to cast Explosion in a place like this, do you?!"

I heard the voice of someone who had pursued me after finishing setting their teleport location, but...

"Explosion——!!"

I unleashed a satisfying Explosion, big enough to reverberate all the way to the palace...!

8

"...Hey, Megumin, starting today, I'm gonna call you the number one idiot of the Crimson Magic Clan."

"If you actually do, I shall call you the loneliest girl of the Crimson Magic Clan," I said, having returned to Axel using Yunyun's Teleport.

"…I could just leave you somewhere, you know?"

"Hey now, you will not get away with leaving me helpless in a busy place like this. What will you do if someone plots something devious, seeing me immobilized after using up all my mana?"

Yunyun was carrying me home on her back.

"Even in a town with as many weirdos as this, the only person I can think of who's contemptible enough to molest you is Kazuma… Ow, ow!"

At her unnecessary comment, I lowered my hand that was around her neck and squeezed her ample pectoral armor as hard as I could.

"Still, I never would have expected it would cause that big a ruckus."

"Why wouldn't you? An announcement came from the capital warning about an assault from the Demon King's army. No matter how you look at it, that was entirely your fault."

"…Well, why not think of it as our thief gang's flashy debut?"

"That makes us more like terrorists! Hey, why don't we disband already? If we keep screwing up, we're probably gonna get an even bigger bounty than the Silver-Haired Thief Brigade."

I wouldn't mind that, either.

"Oh, I'm sure it's fine. Besides, the capital denizens will get used to it—I will be doing this every day from here on, after all."

"Wait just a minute! Why is this the first I'm hearing of this?!"

"Oh, we're about to arrive. My mana has recovered a bit, too. You can let me down here."

"Hey, are you really going to do this again tomorrow? Count me out!"

Ignoring my fellow Crimson Magic Clanner and her fuss, I headed for the mansion…

"…I'm hooome."

"Welcome baaack!" Aqua called from the sofa when I returned to the manor. She was attentively feeding the yellow puffball on her lap.

Just then, I heard angry voices from the kitchen.

"…So your cooking isn't exactly delicious; in fact, it's mediocre! Leave the cooking to me, since I have the skill, and you can just clean up!"

"...I have my pride as a woman, you know! If I lost in cooking to a man who lazes about all day, I wouldn't be able to face the cooks who spent all that time training me when I was young! Just leave it to me—you go relax in the foyer!"

It seemed they were arguing about whose turn it was to prepare food today.

Thrown out of the kitchen, Kazuma came into the room, looking upset.

"Oh? Welcome back, Megumin. Hey, listen, Darkness is whining again..."

Kazuma complained as he sprawled himself out leisurely on the sofa.

"You went and said too much again, didn't you? ...But more importantly... Er, let's make tonight the night..."

"S-sure. Tonight, we'll do that. Yep, tonight's the night for that."

Seemingly unable to come up with tactful phrasing other than "that," Kazuma turned red and stood up.

"What's going on, you two? You're acting strange. What're you talking about?"

"I-it's nothing! It's that thing, that one thing—this morning, Megumin said she was going to form a group or something! Speaking of, how did 'that' go?" Kazuma asked me, trying to change subjects as he panicked under pressure from Aqua.

"It's going surprisingly well. Along with acquiring a hideout today, I recruited two underlings."

"I see. That sounds fun. I'm glad. I often liked making secret bases when I was a kid, too. But if the neighborhood kids steal or destroy your spot, don't make them cry by fighting back."

This guy!

"What kind of person do you think I am?! Anyway, you will be surprised when you see our hideout. It is bigger than this mansion, you see. Plus, I have a new grunt who wields a holy sword and can use legendary-level magic. All in all, it was not a bad outcome for a first day. At this rate, the day we stand shoulder to shoulder with the Silver-Haired Thief Brigade cannot be far."

"I see; that's great. With that holy sword and legendary magic, I bet you'll get along well with your new friend. Just don't go bothering anybody, all right?"

Seriously, how rude can this guy be? Still, explaining that I'm talking about Iris is not an option… Oh well, surely there'll be a chance to tell him about her at some point.

While I pondered, Kazuma suddenly turned to Aqua.

"Hey. I bought some quality liquor today, so feel free to have some. You're always working hard at raising Emperor Zel, after all. So enjoy a bit of booze and take a break once in a while."

"Oh, what in the world's gotten into you? Did you realize you're always doing awful things to me and finally decided to repent? When you put it that way, I'll gladly accept, but I'll stay away from boozing today. I want Megumin to help me come up with a name for Emperor Zel's future special ability. I'll have to save the drinking for another time."

"Huh?! N-no, no! Wouldn't it be better to think about a name after he's actually learned a special ability? Megumin, you must wanna go to bed early after getting tuckered out from all the fun today, too, right? Right?!"

Showing a bit of impatience, Kazuma's voice grew shrill and vehement.

… This guy really seems to think I was just playing around.

I considered explaining to him what actually took place today, but as he wasn't even in our crew, I decided not to tell him yet.

Once our thief gang got much, much bigger, he'd no doubt beg to join. On that day…

"You are right. I'm pretty tired. So once I have eaten, I will go right to bed. Let us fulfill our promise tomorrow."

"Huh?"

I'll tell him about the day I met that masked thief, too.

Chapter 2

The Thief Gang Grows

1

My chanting of Explosion pervaded the grassy hill that overlooked the capital.

"*Explosion—!*"

A streak of light, a thunderous blast.

The capital flew into an uproar, but having used up my mana, I crumpled over, unable to move from that spot.

"Alert! The Demon King's army is attacking! Alert! The Demon King's army is attacking! All adventurers, please gather in front of the royal palace gate right away..."

Just over ten minutes of waiting later, as I was listening detachedly to the announcement being broadcast throughout the capital...

"...Theeeeere you are! You've gotta be kidding me; are you really an idiot?! Hey, are you seriously gonna keep doing this every day?!"

"Sorry I'm late, boss. I managed to escape!"

Perhaps aware that what she was doing was practically a crime, Yunyun was wearing her hood low enough that you couldn't see her face. Her eyes peered out from the dark, glowing red with excitement and anger.

Iris had also arrived, shouldering a small backpack and looking as if she'd gone out for a picnic. The blond princess came running up to where I was lying facedown at the top of the hill.

"Good work, both of you. Er, might you be able to help me up a sec?"

"'Good work,' yourself. Should I just bury you where you lie?! Megumin, you realize the capital is going crazy right now, don't you? What in the world do you plan to do?!"

As Iris flipped me over onto my back, Yunyun started lecturing me with her hands placed on her hips.

"Nothing to be done about it now. You and I have gone through something like this before, remember? Did we not have a similar incident in Crimson Magic Village? Yes, that was a truly heartbreaking day..."

"N-no way do you..."

Yunyun and I had gone through an event comparable to this.

In Crimson Magic Village, a mysterious lady devil who was after Chomusuke had been casting Explosion night after night. The details might be off, but that was the gist of it.

"Do you mean to lay the blame on someone else again?!"

"Wh-what do you mean, 'again'? How rude! If you are talking about the explosions in Crimson Magic Village, that was—without question—the doing of the demoness. As for this time... We could say, *Out of nowhere, there was a Demon King–like figure taking a stroll, and it suddenly cast Explosion and went home*, or something like that as eyewitness information at the police station..."

"I don't think so! I'm not gonna give such stupid testimony!"

As Yunyun went on berating me, Iris took her time and scooped me up in her arms.

"Oh, I had box lunches and snacks made today. There is enough for both of you, so why don't we go somewhere with a good view to eat?"

"Hey, there's more to this girl than just lacking sense, isn't there? She seems like kind of a big deal in the capital!"

While being held, I gave Yunyun instructions.

"We will have people on our heels if we stay here. So let us return to Axel first. I think we should eat the box lunches outside town."

"Who cares about box lunches right now?! Ahhh, that's not what I meant, Illis; please don't look so sad! 'Who cares' was a bit much, sorry. Actually, going on a picnic and eating box lunches with friends is something I've always wanted to do!"

Then, perhaps thanks to Yunyun's shouting, voices aimed at us could be heard coming from town. They were saying things like, "That way," and "Someone's over there."

"Your big mouth got us caught, Yunyun. You are getting too excited over some friends and box lunches. I swear, you forever-alone types! Come on, quick, please cast Teleport!"

"Hey, you think this is my fault?! I'm not sure I'm convinced!"

Though she continued to make a big scene, Yunyun chanted, "*Teleport!*"

She touched us and hurriedly finished the spell.

…Arriving at the lake near Axel, we ate our box lunches on top of a blanket that Iris had been all too happy to spread out.

"Hey, Illis, who made these box lunches? Mmmm, they're so delicious. Um, they're really good, you know, but the ingredients are so fancy. What I mean is, they're not the kind of thing you'd take to a picnic."

"When I said, *'I want to sneak out and have fun with my new friends; won't you help me escape?'* for some reason, my maids were very enthusiastic and put them together."

"Are you saying your home's big enough to have lots of maids? What business are the Chirimendonyas in? I was so happy at the part about new friends that I almost didn't notice, but there were some bits in what you said that I can't just ignore…," Yunyun said, gazing intently at the steamed shark-fin dumpling held between her chopsticks.

"Who cares about such things? There are some things you're better off not asking about, like height or bust size, as well as number of friends and family matters."

"I'm sorry. You're right, Megumin."

Whether because she was convinced or because there was something she didn't want us to ask, Yunyun quietly picked up another morsel from her lunch.

With my mana having recovered enough to eat, I wolfed down the high-end food as I spoke.

"You are quite skilled when it comes to procuring provisions, though, Illis. I hereby appoint you as our supply manager—in other words, a promotion."

"A promotion! Thank you very much. I will do my best!"

"Illis, she just wants you to bring more tasty food; don't let her fool you!"

Having finished our lunch, we went into the lake barefoot and chased around some small fish. We also taught Iris how to skip stones—that's where you throw flat rocks and bounce them off the surface of the lake. We almost nailed someone fishing on the opposite shore and had to apologize profusely.

In the meantime, the day turned to a calm afternoon…

"Today was really fun. I'd love to do this every day. Okay, if we stay too long, someone will probably get worried and come looking for Illis again, so why don't we head back?"

At Yunyun's wistful words, Iris packed the blanket and lunch boxes into her backpack.

"Well then, shall we be off? Today was great fun. Let's come back for another picnic!"

I plodded along after the two of them while they hummed as we headed for Axel…

"No! Why would we go home after we did nothing but eat?! When did this turn into a picnic?! Our work is just beginning!"

Yunyun frowned like she'd had her cover blown.

"Well, boss, what sort of business is on the schedule today?" Iris asked.

I replied, "Right, let us discuss today's plans. The other day, we acquired our hideout. It will be our Axel headquarters… The goal is to create more and more branches all over, eventually expanding our forces on a global scale, but there is something we need first. Therefore, let us procure a source of income so as to build up our funds."

"Hey, you're joking about 'global scale,' right? Sometimes I can't figure out if you're joking or not, Megumin…"

Naturally, I was speaking seriously.

Although…

"Our thief gang already has the Axel HQ and the capital branch. I am sure there will be more and more from here on out. By the way, the hideout in the capital branch is Illis's home. Illis, once we have decided on a symbol for our crew, please make sure you display it up high at your place. Starting today, you are the manager of the capital branch. That is a big promotion."

"Thank you very much. I will do my best!"

"Don't believe her, Illis; she's trying to take over your house!"

It wouldn't be long before our gang's flag flew over the capital castle of this country.

To that end, we first needed some money…

2

"And so please give us work—that is, a long-term and stable moneymaker—that also earns us a good reputation. Something like that would be best."

"Um, why don't you go get a part-time job somewhere?"

We had come to the Adventurers Guild and were asking the receptionist lady for some solid work.

Iris, eyes sparkling, observed the adventurers in the Guild as I refused to waver at the fast and cold reply.

"I want something more, you know, appropriate for us, not a job like that. The three of us are confident in our abilities, get it? Like, when something turns up and threatens the town, we defeat it and receive a protection fee—that sort of work..."

"I heard a security firm started doing similar things just the other day, but they went out of business in the blink of an eye, you know?"

For some reason, Yunyun, who was right next to me, averted her eyes at the receptionist's words.

Did she know something about this security firm that went under?

"In any case, giving dangerous work to three young girls is just..."

So she was judging us on our appearances.

We'd already had trouble getting members because of how we looked.

"Please, lady, it's okay if it doesn't rake in cash! Please give us some work that will continually win us money and the adoration of the townsfolk. That way they'll want to join our crew! Also, if possible, combat-related work would be great!"

"Work that fits those conditions is not something you see very oft— Ah."

The lady made a small noise, as if she knew something about a job fitting those exact specifications.

"What is it? Is there something? Please let us do that, then!"

"No. Well, there is, but it's already taken, you could say... Actually, it's a quest for slaying the crows that have been getting into the town's trash collection sites. I don't know why, but someone offered to do it for free."

Slaying crows.

It certainly would earn the townspeople's gratitude, it was technically combat-related, and it had the potential to earn us some steady money, but...

Yeah, Crimson Magic Clan members and a princess heading out to slay crows was unthinkable.

It was what you'd call a waste of talent—overkill.

"That sort of quest definitely isn't what I had in mind. The day I get a nickname as embarrassing as Crow Slayer, I will no longer be able to hold my head high as a proud member of my clan. Do you not have anything else? It doesn't have to be from the town. Is there a big store or group somewhere that can give us regular work?"

The lady thought hard for a while at my question.

"Well, I suppose there is technically a place that meets your conditions…"

…On the outskirts of Axel, in front of a moderately sized church that looked like it had recently been remodeled.

"I never thought we would end up back here…"

"Hey, Megumin, let's forget about this. This is one place we shouldn't go in!"

This was the Axis Church's branch in Axel.

"What a pretty blue chapel, and just built, too! …Are you not going in?"

Apparently, not knowing much about the Axis Church, Iris alone had made some naive remarks as she looked up at the building.

"Illis, this is a very troublesome and dangerous place. If the people in here try anything funny, I give you permission to attack."

"This time, at least, Megumin's right, okay, Illis? If any weirdos jump out, you don't need to hold back."

With that warning, Iris, her head cocked, quietly opened the church door…

At the same time, there came the sound of something falling over and shattering.

"Ahhh, the expensive vase I put in front of the door! The vase rumored to bring happiness just by having it! Breaking something like this is like trying to steal my happiness, you impudent jerk! Now you'll have to take responsibility and choose whether to look after me, pay to replace it, or join the Axis Church… Oh, Megumin and Yunyun?"

Giving a feverish whirlwind rant, the priestess looked stunned upon seeing us standing at the entrance.

"Um, we came here on a commission from the Guild… But maybe we will just be going."

Cecily's face lit up upon hearing my reply.

*   *   *

"...Er, do we really not need to pay for it? I would think such an incredible vase would be quite an expensive and powerful magical item..."

Moved to tears at seeing Iris's apologetic face, Cecily clasped her hands together to pray.

...No, she'd been offering a prayer before that.

"Ahhh, thank you, Lady Aqua! That you would send me such an innocent loli...!"

Cecily seemed to be in high spirits today, no longer even listening to the talk of our quest.

It might've been better to just go home pretending nothing had happened.

"Illis, this woman deliberately placed that vase in front of the door, so you need not worry about it. She was waiting for someone to come in and break it. It is a nasty way to swindle someone out of a lot of money or push them into joining this Church by placing the blame on them."

I explained Cecily's methods to Iris, who still looked troubled.

Upon hearing my explanation, the blond princess curiously gave Cecily a look of reverence.

"I never would have thought to get money or followers that way. You must be very smart, Cecily!"

"Illis, that's not something to admire! What this woman does is borderline criminal, do you understand?!"

Actually, I think it's past borderline. It's just straight-up criminal.

"Your name is Illis, right? I'm Cecily, a distinguished and beautiful priestess of the Axis Church. Feel free to call me Big Sis."

"Certainly, nice to meet you, Big Sis. My name is Illis."

"Hff, hff." Cecily started breathing slowly and heavily after hearing the cute girl obediently call her that nickname.

"Hey, Megumin, could it be that tomorrow is the day I perish? Will I die, having used up all my life's good luck on this blessed day?"

"You're satisfied with your life because of something like this? Illis, this woman is going to become unstable, so just call her Cecily instead."

"Ahhh, no!"

The priestess was experiencing some kind of disappointed shock. I decided to force a change of topic, since the conversation wasn't going anywhere.

"Well, back to what I was saying… We came here on a commission from the Guild. May I discuss business with you?"

As Cecily wrapped her arms around her knees, depressed and starting to sulk, I showed her the quest bulletin we got from the Guild.

3

"Well then, let us get down to it. Though it is actually not that hard a job. The details are exactly as the paper says."

Basically, the job amounted to two tasks. The first was finding and driving away a shady person who'd been coming around the church recently. The other was a call for salesgirls, in order to procure a source of money for the church.

Suspicious-person identification aside, the salesgirl part was quite a cushy gig.

Apparently, all we had to do was regularly show up a few times a month for just a few hours.

Doing that alone, supposedly we would receive a tenth of all sales.

On the posting, it had been written that an interview was mandatory for the salesgirl job, but according to Cecily, that wasn't necessary for us.

I didn't know what they wanted to sell, but as far as terms and conditions, you could say this was pretty unusual.

"The salesgirl job looks like a piece of cake, so that sounds good. By the way, about the other bit of work…"

At my query, Cecily put a finger to her cheek and looked troubled.

"Well, it's something that's been going on for a little while, and…"

According to Cecily's explanation, someone had been eating the garden veggies growing behind the chapel and stealing food from the fridge inside.

She also said the perpetrator made no sound, and by the time she'd noticed, the food was already gone. However, when she asked people in the neighborhood, nobody had seen anyone questionable.

"A veggie thief and fridge raiding? I'm not quite sure what their aim is. If it's to steal food, they surely would not need to go out of their way to steal it from such a dangerous church. There ought to be safer and easier places to hit. If they got caught here…who knows what would happen to them?"

"Megumin, I don't think our church is that unscrupulous. I don't know of anyone who hates it."

I was racking my brain, trying to figure out who the culprit was, when Yunyun timidly opened her mouth.

"Maybe this is some kind of grudge, Megumin? Like, somebody who was wronged by the Axis Church is coming to exact their revenge…"

"A grudge? …Cecily, do you remember ever doing anything somebody would hold animosity over? Even something small?"

At that, the priestess looked up at the ceiling, trying to remember.

"…I don't know, really," she said, sadly shaking her head a bit.

My prejudice that a priestess of the Axis Church had to be hated by someone might have made me speak a bit rudely.

"I see. Sorry for asking something a little tasteless. Well, you might have unknowingly annoyed someone who now hates you despite your good intentions…"

"No, that's not what I mean. I remember so many grudges from people, I guess I can't hope to narrow it down…"

"That is disappointing; please give back my apology! What in the world did you do? Come on—let's have you apologize to everyone you remember!"

In the end, Cecily was exactly who I thought she was.

"Still, it is strange for there to be no witnesses with such frequent thefts. Is the time of the crime always the same?"

"I'm not sure about the time, since I usually realize I've been robbed after the fact…"

The priestess pondered as she exchanged glances with Yunyun.

"Cecily, what is your relationship with your neighbors like? Maybe you screwed up again, and your neighbors are conspiring against you…"

"I work hard to get along with my neighbors here. In my old town, I often had trouble with them, and there was even a big hullabaloo where they came close to evicting me."

Really, though, what are we gonna do with this girl?

"In any case, we will not get anywhere without any clues. Why don't we defer the criminal search and hear about what we'll be selling in the salesgirl job?"

Hearing that, Cecily gleefully went to the back of the chapel and returned hugging something.

It was a box full of a large amount of white powder.

"…Ummm. Cecily, is this perhaps—?"

Before I could ask what it was, the priestess held up a finger.

"*Shh!* Megumin, you mustn't say any more. This is simply powder that makes you very happy just by putting it into your mouth."

"Huh?!"

Yunyun looked shocked at what she heard, while Iris cocked her head, confused.

"Cecily, this is contraband, is it not? You will get in trouble again if you are found out, you know?"

"'Again'?! By 'again,' you mean she's been convicted before?!"

While Yunyun commented each step of the way, Iris's eyebrows perked up at the word *contraband*.

"Hee-hee, it's fine, Megumin. It's not *that*. This is a special product, using you-know-what as a base with repeated improvements. It isn't banned yet. It's already confirmed to cause no harm to the human body. Hee-hee-hee, once they know about this, none of the people in this town will be able to resist it!"

"!"

As Cecily smiled suspiciously, Yunyun drew her wand from her hip. My fellow Crimson Magic Clanner wore a sad look while she pointed it at the priestess.

"Cecily, you talk and act strange sometimes, but I didn't think you were the sort of person to do this! You're just not someone I can over-look. I will make you reform!"

Yunyun seemed to be seriously misunderstanding. Iris followed suit and smoothly drew her sword.

"Anything designated as contraband must be harmful to this coun-try. Even if it's a special improved version, I cannot let it slide!"

"Wait, why are the two of you looking at your big sis so coldly?! If I did something wrong, I'll apologize. Look, I'll even make sure to share this with both of you!"

Cecily became horribly flustered at the sudden turn of events.

"I can't believe you would offer you-know-what to us... Surely you never offered it to Megumin or anything?"

"Huh?! ...W-well, of course I tried to share the joy of this you-know-what with..."

Yunyun's eyes glowed red.

Strange, I've somehow seen a turn of events just like this before.

"Wait! Could you listen to what Big Sis Cecily has to say?! I think you've got the wrong idea!"

The two of them slowly crept toward the priestess.

"You seem to be confused. This is a candy currently banned for sale because kids and old people can easily get it stuck in their throats. It's gelatinous-slime powder," I said.

""Huh?""

Weapons still in hand, both of them stopped in their tracks upon hearing that.

"*Sob, sob...* This you-know-what is a revolutionary special product that won't get stuck in Grandpa's throat when he eats it..."

The two of them exchanged glances as Cecily sobbed.

4

"...I swear! I would never sell something sinister! You realize I am part of the clergy, right?"

""Sorry!""

With the tables turned and Cecily now assertively lecturing them, Iris and Yunyun apologized in unison.

Though I still felt like Cecily was to blame for using confusing phrasing each and every step of the way.

"This you-know-what is a revolutionary special product that won't get stuck in your throat. I spent a lot of time working on it. However, if we put it up for sale under the same 'gelatinous slime,' the police will come. So why don't we call it 'Axis Church's White Powder'?"

"I think that name is way more likely to make the cops come."

After talking it over a bit, we settled on the name "Axis Church's You-Know-What."

Did she really intend to sell this stuff? Was it even something people would buy?

Unconcerned with such thoughts, Cecily said, "Well then, let's get to it! With all of you here, you can bet this will sell like crazy!" and cheerfully lifted up a box of the you-know-what.

...I knew I had a bad feeling about this.

"Boss? Is it okay for us to take so much money for work like this, just passing out powder? It seems like a terribly simple job somehow," Iris said with a mystified look while she handed a customer some of the you-know-what.

I did the same with another patron.

"The work itself is simple and easy, so you're not wrong. However, we have the right to receive a high-enough compensation."

I then glanced over at Cecily.

"Come and get Axis Church's You-Know-What! My church made this with a technique we can't really talk about! It's super easy to use. You just mix it with water and eat it! It's goopy and slimy and oh, will you love it! Come now—won't you taste some of the you-know-what those pretty little girls have in their hands?"

I gotta say, this is a failure. A failure in so many ways.

Why did she always have to make it sound so suspicious?

Yunyun stood next to me, blushing at the phrasing, but nevertheless doing her job, handing the substance to patrons who came by.

There'd been mention of an interview for salesgirls, but apparently, this was what it referred to.

Attractive young women handing out packets of powder.

That was all we were doing, but…

"Excuse me, that there's that banned stuff, right?"

"Oh, not at all, sir. This has been improved to meet safety standards, making it non-banned you-know-what. Come on! I'm sure you will find it utterly addicting!"

"I'll take some! I'll take three packs!"

Despite the questionable solicitations, the young man went out of his way to buy you-know-what from each of us.

"Just asking, Cecily, but this really is just an improved version of gelatinous slime, right? One that goes down smooth and tasty when you eat it, right?"

"Yup. I don't know what else it could be, Megumin, but you're correct."

With the phrasing she and the customer had used, it all felt dubious to me.

"Come one, come all! It's you-know-what, squeezed hard by embarrassed pretty little girls! If you buy now, it's only… Oh, is that…?"

"Hmm? Funny meeting you here, Cecily. Long time no see."

An old gentleman passing by called to the priestess upon seeing her. They seemed to know each other.

"Ooh, could it be…?! Is that what I think it is? The stuff that gives you a taste of heaven when you mix it with hot water and do you-know-what…?!"

"Yes, by doing that even more to the you-know-what, we have greatly reduced its effects on the human body. As kindred aficionados, allow me to share a bit with y—"

"This is gelatinous slime, right?! This is really just contraband gelatinous slime, is it not?!"

""Shh!""

Unable to stand it any longer, I yelled and was unjustly silenced for some reason.

5

In the end, the you-know-what, despite being scandalous in so many ways, sold out in the blink of an eye.

Lewd and perilous phrasings had abounded, but I still couldn't hide my surprise at learning of gelatinous slime's unexpected popularity.

Gleeful upon getting back to the church, Cecily praised our efforts.

"The three of you did splendidly! Next time, it would be even better if you could mix the you-know-what with hot water and slurp it down in front of everyone…"

"I will not! Hey, Megumin, we're not gonna do jobs like this anymore, are we?! I really felt like I was doing something scandalous today, in more ways than one…," Yunyun said, looking as if she'd lost something important.

Regardless, this job let us make good money in a short time. Surely, there was no reason not to continue.

"Miss Cecily, I had a lot of fun today! I earned money for the first time!"

"Ah, wait a second, Illis! D-don't look at your big sis like that! It somehow makes me want to repent to Lady Aqua!"

Cecily clutched her own body, writhing under Iris's innocent gaze.

Before long, Cecily said she'd feed everyone some of the slime and fled toward the kitchen…

"Ahhh! They did it again!"

A sudden cry came our way.

…Following where Cecily had gone, we searched the area to look for clues.

"There was food in there before we left the church, right?"

"Yes, I'm certain. I was keeping the gelatinous-slime powder in here; I saw how much food was stored at the time."

We'd been out selling for only around an hour, so the theft had to have occurred recently.

I didn't know how much food they'd taken, but it seemed unlikely they'd have been able to do it this skillfully unless they'd been watching the church, waiting for us to leave.

Just then, Iris suddenly exclaimed, "Look, Cecily, footprints! Something was clearly being dragged—might it be from the person who took the food?"

Taking a look, I saw there were absolutely traces of someone pressing something oily against the floor and dragging it.

Peering, the priestess gave a solemn nod and said, "The other day, in the middle of making tempura, I fell and knocked over the pot. I remember casting Heal on myself and crawling around while writhing and covered in oil."

What exactly was this person doing with her life?

Opening the magic fridge, Yunyun seemed to find something.

"Miss Cecily, look at this! For some reason, there's, um, men's underwear in the fridge! If the culprit put something like this in the fridge of a church where a woman lives, they're definitely a pervert!"

Looking inside the magic device, I indeed saw some chilled underwear stored within.

Clearly, as another woman, Yunyun couldn't let such sexual harassment fly.

She took the underwear and crushed them in anger.

Again, the priestess nodded solemnly.

"A male worshipper who doesn't have a refrigerator at home left those in there. Apparently, he can't relax after a soak unless he puts on cold underwear, so he stops by every day on his way home from the public baths."

As Yunyun hurled the underwear away, Cecily raised her voice in determination.

"We're getting nowhere. Megumin, now that it's come to this, let's interrogate each and every person who might bear ill will against me! All you have to do is make your eyes glow red and twirl your staff behind me. Then I will say, *You have something to say to me, don't you? If you don't spit it out, I don't know what the Crimson Magic Clansperson behind me will do…*"

"I will not cooperate with your threats! Just have a proper talk with them, please!"

…Our first suspect was the butcher. His was apparently the closest shop to the Axis church.

"All right, out with it! When I asked for 'meat the same softness as a fourteen-year-old girl's cheeks,' you said, 'Never heard of it.' You were disgusted, weren't you? Later, when I spread the rumor about you being useless and knowing nothing about good meat, you got mad and turned to crime…"

"Hey, wait a minute, after you wasted my time with that idiotic order of yours, you went and spread rumors?! Let's go to the police; I'm turning you in for obstruction of business!"

"Ahhh, w-wait a minute, please. Don't involve the cops! Recently, there's this charming young man at the station who looks at me condescendingly and says, 'You again?!' At least wait till after I check if he has a girlfriend…!"

…Maybe I should just leave her and go home?

When I looked at Yunyun, she nodded quickly, as if she understood what I was thinking for once.

All right, time to go home.

"…Excuse me, sir, please wait. I will apologize, too, so please forgive Cecily."

A pure and innocent young girl's voice cut through the unusual atmosphere of the conversation.

"E-er. I mean, well, the, uh, maybe the police thing was a bit much. L-look. I'll forgive you for this girl's sake, but don't go doing that again." The butcher spoke with finality and then turned away. He had been unable to resist Iris's pleading eyes.

The criminal priestess, watching the man lumber back to his shop, was on the verge of tears as she grabbed Iris.

"Ooohhh, Illis, thank youuuuu! In return, Big Sis will make you her li'l sis!"

"N-no, um, about that… I just recently got a new big bro, so…"

Dang, there goes our chance to ditch, I thought a bit regretfully while watching Iris, at a loss for what to do.

"That was close. His leading interrogation did me in."

"Miss Cecily, was it not your own mouth that got you in trouble?" Having recovered, Cecily paid no heed to my observation.

"Next is over there! Yes, the idea to go round-robin starting nearby was a big mistake! I should have begun the questioning with the most likely candidate!" The priestess ran off without even waiting for our reply.

"She's very proactive…"

That may have been Iris's impression, but I thought Cecily was being more thoughtless than proactive.

"…Megumin, maybe we should've gone home after eating lunch today after all."

For today, at least, I was willing to concede that much.

6

We chased after Cecily, and sure enough, she had gone after the Axis Church's sworn enemy.

"Yo, come out right now, you Eris Church losers! Gimme back the pudding I was saving!"

K-thnk, k-thnk! Cecily was kicking the rival Church's door.

"You mustn't look, Illis! Shield your eyes. Grow to be a purehearted woman."

Trying to keep her from seeing what Cecily was doing, Yunyun covered Iris's eyes while standing behind the young princess.

"Miss Cecily, what are you doing? I know you are on bad terms with the Eris Church, but this is taking it too far."

Even when I tried to drag her back home, Cecily started pounding *bam-bam* on the door and refused to leave.

That was when…

"Are you here again?! How many times do we have to ask you not to come back before you understand?!"

The door opened, and an Eris priestess emerged.

…After we explained everything, the priestess let out a deep sigh.

"You know, we're always healing adventurers' wounds or distributing food. We don't have the spare time to head over to your church. Besides, we aren't particularly in need of things to eat. Why would the servants of Lady Eris engage in theft?"

"Liar! If you really weren't hurting for food, you wouldn't have looked at me the way you did when I made a show of biting into a kebab in front of you the other day!"

"You did?" the lady of the Eris Church muttered in disgust and, curiously, winced briefly. "The Eris Church holds that poverty is virtuous. Someone eating kebabs in front of us wouldn't exactly—"

"Oh, another fib! You looked pretty worried when I told you followers of Eris wouldn't get big boobs because they don't eat enough protein!"

"Wh-why, you! Now you've said it, heathen!"

They started fighting, and as I pulled them apart, I found myself scolding the two.

"I know you both are in different sects, but why do two clergywomen have to fight all the time?"

Perhaps embarrassed that she'd sunk to Cecily's level, the Eris priestess turned red.

"Er… W-well, that is… I'm so embarrassed…"

"Ha-ha! Take that!"

"That goes for you, too, Cecily!"

As I expressed my disgust with the woman from the Axis Church, she continued to run down her mental list of potential criminals.

"But if this boob-stuffing priestess doesn't know, then who…? I have so many other people in mind, I really can't figure out who did it…"

"If you don't stop, I'm going to get a mace and rough up your church."

After forcing Cecily to apologize to the Eris Church priestess, who was now trying to hide her chest, we went on our way.

Was this really someone seeking revenge?

If the Eris follower's reaction was anything to go on, most people didn't want anything to do with the Axis Church.

So would anyone really go for payback just because of a little annoyance?

"Why don't we go back to the chapel one more time?" I suggested to Cecily, whom Yunyun and Iris were busy stopping from trying to graffiti the Eris Church's sign.

"...They did it again," Cecily muttered while sinking to the floor.

"What's the damage? It doesn't look like as much is gone this time..."

Ignoring Cecily, who had collapsed in front of the fridge, I peeked inside. There didn't seem to be that big of a difference.

"The gelatinous slime I stored farther back is gone... Just how many times has this happened now...? They're even aiming straight for my favorite foods—perhaps this is the work of the Demon King's army?"

"I don't want to think about the Demon King's army stealing snacks out of some church's fridge, but there is a certain something I am wondering about."

It was the evidence of dragging something that Iris had first spotted.

The marks went from the kitchen out to the rear door of the church.

As I recalled, the culprit had stolen from the church refrigerator and the garden out back.

I opened the rear door with a *wham*, and...!

"...Um, Cecily. A gelatinous slime is eating your veggies."

"Ahhh, what?! You're right! The slime I thought I strangled is happily wolfing down my...! Could it be that Lady Aqua has granted this miracle?!"

"Cecily, no matter what way you look at it, this slime is the culprit, is it not?! Please apologize to the people you accused!"

*   *   *

"…That was an…unpleasant incident, huh…?"

The culprit had turned out to be a slime that Cecily had made some extreme modifications to, causing its Vitality to rise.

Yunyun and I scolded the priestess, whose eyes showed not even a hint of regret. Eventually, Iris stopped us.

"I swear, you need to learn a bit more about Axis followers. I know you are naive, but wow."

"Even so, I don't think Cecily is that bad of a person… I have a good eye for character."

About as good as Aqua's.

However, something seemed off about Cecily as I laid into her.

She was trembling rhythmically as she sat on the floor…

"Illis, you most definitely should join the Axis Church! Yes, very much so!"

"Illis, let us go home for the day. It was a mistake to bring you here to begin with. We will not come around here again, so please forget everything that happened today."

As if taking Iris away from the palace wasn't bad enough, if it got out that she'd been made to join the Axis Church when I wasn't looking, I'd be executed for sure.

"Cecily, I don't know anything about the Axis Church's teachings—what sort of things does it preach, exactly?"

"What a good question! Illis, is there anything you're suppressing about yourself? In the teachings of our Church, we mainly believe that self-restraint is a poison to the body, so you should live exactly as you want. Do as you please. Insist on having things your way. If you love someone, no matter how high their station in life, don't hold back. Instead, go after them so hard that you force them down to your own level."

"Don't listen! Here, plug your ears!"

Yunyun covered Iris's ears to protect the princess from Cecily's gleeful sermon.

That was when something interrupted us.

The front door burst open, and a voice I recognized called from outside.

"I heard a sweet little blond-haired, blue-eyed girl had been brought here. Stay calm and do not resist, everyone... Ahhh, Lady Illis! I found you!"

Standing there was Claire, the white-suited female bodyguard. Seeing her, Iris looked down and sulked, dejected.

"Is it time to go already...?"

"Lady Illis, it's not 'time to go'! I don't remember ever allowing you to stroll about outside to begin with!"

While the royal bodyguard berated Iris, who seemed to have gotten used to life on the outside, Cecily slipped in a bit closer.

"Erm, who might you be? Nice to meet you; I am the priestess in charge here. My name is Cecily, the Axis Church's Axel branch manager. I have shown Illis here every hospitality, please rest assured." Cecily spoke unusually coolly. It was a very uncharacteristic display of sincerity for an Axis follower. I was sure *she* had been the one we were showing every kindness.

"Huh? A-ah, well, thank you." Seeming to have taken the bait, Claire looked confused for a moment before continuing. "I am Claire, responsible for guarding Lady Illis. Thank you very much for safeguarding her in my absence. So responsible people number among the Axis Church's ranks as well," she said, straightening her posture and bowing her head deeply.

I knew this woman was hot-tempered; she'd even tried to slash at Kazuma before. Apparently, if it was for Iris's sake, she could also be quite respectful.

Then, in the middle of my quiet admiration:

"I see, so you are Illis's bodyguard... I was just in the middle of teaching her the precepts of the Axis Church. What do you say? As her guardian, by all means, I invite you join in."

"The Axis Church?! N-no, something like that would be a big scand— I mean, Lady Illis isn't even an adult yet, so something like that could pose a problem. Or, uhhh... Lady Illis has to have a fair and balanced perspective to begin with, so it would be an issue if she devoted herself to a certain sect right away, ummm…"

Perhaps unable to assert herself against a wise clergywoman, Claire tried to refuse, but…

"You would be perfect as an Axis follower. I can tell—you have the comrade scent."

"Th-the 'comrade scent'…?" Looking a bit disgusted, Claire sniffed her sleeves.

"Are you suffering from a forbidden love? Do you have impermissible feelings for someone? In the Axis Church, you can be with anyone, even if they're the same sex or of a different rank, as long as they're not undead or a devil child."

"Even if they're the same sex or of a different rank?! Th-th-that… No, but…"

Claire was awfully shaken, as if something about the tenets had struck a chord with her.

"Come, now—suppression is a poison to the body, you know? Restraint violates the Axis precepts. Do as you wish. As you feel…!"

"Ahhh, I—I must be going for today! Lady Illis, please say your good-byes!"

Apparently thinking it'd be a bad idea to stick around any longer, Claire took her charge's hand and left the church in a flustered panic.

"…Well then, boss, Yunyun, Cecily, see you tomorrow!"

"No, you will not! I won't let you—I'll watch you all day tomorrow!"

Iris, who should have been dejected at being taken home, now looked cheerful, waving at us while Claire led her away.

"…She was biting, and I let her slip away…," Cecily muttered regretfully.

Had Illis been the one biting or Claire?

It frightened me to think that either may have joined after just one more good push.

"Hey, Megumin, that Claire lady said, 'Lady Illis has to have a fair and balanced perspective,' so does that mean Illis is…?" Yunyun started but then shook her head, seeming to think it impossible.

Leaving the other Crimson Magic Clan member aside, I turned to the priestess.

"Cecily."

"I wish you'd go back to calling me Big Sis…"

As always, the woman insisted on having things her own way.

"Actually, I would like to continue earning money, not just as a onetime gig."

"That works out for me, too. I have lots of different ideas for making money besides Axis Church's You-Know-What. 'Rice Balls Made By Pretty Little Girls,' 'Balloons Inflated By Pretty Little Girls,' 'Pretty Little Girls'…"

"Are not all of those just exploiting young women?! I would prefer to earn money a bit more respectably, if possible…"

"Hee-hee-hee," Cecily giggled at me blithely.

"Do you want to make money so badly because of something to do with Illis?"

She was usually so thoughtless, yet now this woman seemed to be looking straight into my mind.

"Well, you might say it has a bit to do with her. If we can procure stable funding and grow our organization enough, I believe it is no mere fantasy that we could someday help a certain masked thief defeat the Demon King…"

"'Defeat the Demon King'—you're thinking big again!"

Yes, surely it was more than mere imagination.

I couldn't help but think that easygoing masked bandit was capable of felling such a powerful foe.

Also, if he could defeat the Demon King…

"In a peaceful world without the Demon King, I figure that girl would be freer to go out and about than she is now."

Then I would be able to invite her to picnics, like today, or do anything else with her. I was sure she'd be delighted, too.

"I am no good at making money, so will you help me? You seem to be good at coming up with unusual ways to earn cash."

Really, I could've just asked a certain guy, but… Well, I wanted to brag to him a bit after my gang had grown a little more.

Yunyun didn't particularly seem to object to relying on this confounded priestess, either, and nodded just a bit happily.

However…

"I can't accept that so easily."

Shaking her head as if to say she wouldn't be tricked by such sympathetic words, Cecily continued. "I am an Axis follower who loves lolis more than anything else. Megumin, if you, Yunyun, and Illis are doing something that interesting…then let me into that shady group of yours, too! I'll agree to anything!" The woman's eyes lit up as she said something incredibly stupid.

7

"…I'm home!"

"Hey, welcome back, Megumin. Tonight's dinner was prepared by the skillful hands of yours truly! Look forward to it!"

Darkness's cockiness greeted me when I returned to the mansion.

Kazuma, who was lazily sprawled out on the sofa in the foyer, said, "Megumin, can you get her to stop? All I did was make one little complaint about her cooking yesterday. Now this girl is being a huge pain. She's been saying today's the day she's gonna show me what for, or whatever."

"Don't call me a pain! You were the one making fun of me! You just wait and see, 'cause I am technically a woman, and my cooking's not gonna lose to some NEET's!"

While Darkness withdrew into the kitchen in a huff, Kazuma shouted, "Hey, Darkness, I'm not a fan of that watery stuff you made yesterday! It may be fancy, but junk food is what I like. I wanna eat something greasy today."

"Greasy, huh...? I already made something, but oh well, I'll whip up another dish. I swear, you should make your requests sooner—"

That's when Aqua interrupted.

"I like food that's light. Something that you can just, like, slurp down would be nice."

"'Slurp down'... Ummm, you mean noodles? *Erg*, oh well, I'll start those, too... Wh-what about you, Megumin?"

Having gotten an extra order from Aqua, too, Darkness now asked me for requests.

"You already made something, right? I'm fine with that—your cooking is average, but not exactly a failure anyway."

"Don't call me 'average,' Megumin! Still, it helps not to get an order that's off-the-wall. I'll go prepare the additional dishes, so hold on a sec."

After Darkness returned to the kitchen, Aqua brought a board game over to Kazuma as he lay on the sofa.

"Kazuma, Kazuma, play with me while dinner's cooking. Things will be different this time; I have a secret plan up my sleeve, after all."

With words that so obviously foreshadowed defeat, she giddily set up the pieces.

"What do you mean, you 'have a secret plan' up your sleeve? The other day you said the same thing. When it came down to it, you shouted, 'There's no time limit, so I'm stalling! I may be no match in a battle of wits, but I won't lose a test of endurance! I'm gonna take so much time that we could be here all night, so do your worst!' and then you fell asleep ten minutes later."

"Shut it! That was then; this is now. Hee-hee, this time I've really got something amazing in store. You can go first. Come on—go ahead."

Kazuma moved a piece against Aqua, who was brimming with confidence.

"You fell for it, Kazuma! I, in my wisdom, had the idea to deliberately go second and make the exact same moves as my opponent! In other words, my opponent will face someone just as strong as themselves.

However, I am doing more than just copying—yes, although we'd be equally matched by mirroring my opponent's skill, what happens when my skill is added on top?"

Self-assured, Aqua made the exact same move as Kazuma.

"Yes, this revolutionary tactic is my fearsome secret plan, and with it, I can win against anyone! All I have to do is imitate my opponent's moves without even thinking. The instant they eventually tire out and make a mistake, I just have to start trying for real and…!"

Aqua stopped mid-sentence. It seemed she was already in a pickle. Saying she'd imitate her opponent only got her outmaneuvered.

Ignoring Aqua, who was busy strategizing, I took Chomusuke into my arms as she brushed against my feet, and gave a report of the day's events.

"Kazuma, we had pretty good results today. First, we succeeded in procuring a stable source of income for our crew's future endeavors. With this, you could say we've taken a big step toward our goal."

He listened to my words without taking his eyes off the game.

"That's great. What, so by 'procuring a stable source of income,' you mean you were working a part-time job?"

"Yes, more or less. We killed slimes and whatnot—a commission from the Guild."

He slapped a piece down and said, "Slime hunting, huh? Well, stuff like that might not be dangerous for your level, but if the other girls get in trouble, be sure to help them out, all right? Oh, guess that's check already."

"Come on—that makes no sense. How am I the one at a disadvantage when I'm making the same moves?"

It seemed he still thought I was just playing pretend. Maybe he just thought I was exterminating slimes with the neighborhood kids?

Oh well.

Telling him about it after we were huge, big enough to make him shake in his boots, was going to be great.

"Dinner's ready, everyone. No one is going to complain about my food today. Well, come sit down!"

As I helped Darkness put dinner on the table, I said, "Speaking of—one more thing."

I turned to Kazuma, who was finishing up a quick counterattack to Aqua's move. He hadn't even considered the play at all.

"I got another member."

The
Thief
Gang
Strays

Chapter
3

1

…Things were going well.

On the thief gang's very first day, I had acquired a secret ba—I mean, a hideout to serve as our stronghold, as well as a powerful grunt for some muscle.

Plus, just the other day, I succeeded in getting regular pocket mon—I mean, a regular source of income for the crew and added someone who could use Heal to our ranks.

Honestly, I'd never expected it to go so well.

Or rather, I had a hunch our gang would get bigger than I'd originally anticipated.

The reason was that—

"…Megumin, guess what, guess what! I sent a letter to the Axis Church headquarters about our thief gang. Apparently, they've been flooded with applicants. This might be a chance to expand our forces," said Cecily, who'd cheekily brought her things and moved into Axel's number one mansion with us. The priestess looked as if she thought she was the master of the place.

"…Axis followers? Um, let me think on that just a bit."

Cecily lay about on the expensive-looking sofa she'd claimed. Something about her reminded me of Aqua.

If all Axis followers were like this, I kind of wanted to deny them entry.

"After I wrote saying it was comprised of only lolis, excepting me, apparently there was even a quarrel when Lord Zesta said he'd quit as high priest and join. If you're ever in trouble, the Axis Church will always be there for you, see?"

"Th-thank you. If anything should happen, then by all means."

A sudden wave of fatigue hit me, and it wasn't just from my post-Explosion lack of mana this time.

I sank my body into the sofa like Cecily. Yunyun, who was reading some letter, fidgeted while she said to me, "E-er, Megumin? I sent my dad a letter, too. I got a reply saying lots of people in Crimson Magic Village want in 'cause it sounds cool and fun…"

"…No, everyone in the Crimson Magic Clan has the important job of watching the Demon King's castle. To begin with, they are like an ace-in-the-hole fighting force for when the capital has an emergency, so they must not come to a place like this."

It wasn't like the village wasn't strong enough. Sure, they'd be perfect for invading the Demon King's castle, but our enemies were just crooked nobles. Also, we were going to be chivalrous thieves, not burglars.

"That's true; I was just giddy about getting more companions. Well then, I'll reply asking for help if we're ever in trouble."

"S-sure, if that ever happens, then I suppose there's no harm…"

While I evaded the issue, the forever-alone girl smiled in delight, more about getting companions than anything else.

I sure did have a feeling our gang would get bigger than I'd originally anticipated.

Yes, and the reason was…

"When I bragged to my father the other day about forming a group for justice, he said if we didn't have enough hands, I could take as many skilled knights as we needed. He also said that should we need money, I was to take as much as I like! Boss, if you ever need help, please ask me anytime!"

...Yep, things were going really well.

But somehow, I felt like the gang was getting to be a bigger group than I'd envisioned.

2

And so.

"I cannot exactly look over this entire list the three of you gave me. Actually, in numbers alone, this is already more than some knight or mercenary orders. We talked before about our goal being to help the Silver-Haired Thief Brigade from the shadows while they forge their own way regardless of the bounty on their heads, but the shadows can't possibly hold this many people."

Having rested for a bit, my mana had recovered enough to move, and I glanced over the bundle of papers my followers had given me.

It included Axis followers, Crimson Magic Clansfolk, and even knights and competent adventurers who were famous in the capital.

Our goal was to be a small, elite thief gang, just like my idols.

That wasn't to say I had gotten cold feet from something that started on a whim getting out of hand so quickly.

As I politely explained this, Yunyun got a silly grin on her face.

"...Hey, if you have something to say, let's hear it."

"I would neeever. I certainly wasn't thinking that you always wimp out when things don't go the way you plan, Megumin."

As I prepared an assault on the impossibly lonely girl who thought she knew everything about people, Iris interjected in a shaky voice. "Boss, I understand what you're saying, but why don't we at least let a few more people join? We have two wizards and one priestess. I can use my sword and magic, so I'll act as an attacker for our party, but I would like at least one more fighter."

"It's not like we're going to go on a monster-hunting adventure, so we don't really need to have a balanced party, you know? Actually, we already have more than enough power to raid a nobleman's mansion anyway."

We had two Crimson Magic Clan Arch-wizards and even a super-overpowered princess who was the descendant of a hero.

I wasn't sure about the other one, but in the worst-case scenario, she'd help us plenty just by being there as a healer. Iris still looked troubled, however.

"Er, why don't we go on adventures sometimes? I'd like to have someone below me anyway. Forever being the grunt isn't very..."

"...Well, that lonely girl there seems to have a spark of hope in her eyes for adventuring, too, so I will think about it. Though, do you really desire a newcomer for such a silly reason? Oh well, I'll promote you to being my left hand, so please be patient. By the way, Yunyun is my right hand. So congrats—you're the number three in our lineup."

Left hand or right, they got neither pay nor benefits, so saying as much was free.

Not to mention, there were only four of us, so being number three didn't get you anything, either, but Iris was genuinely delighted.

No matter how powerful she was, she was a kid, after all.

Surprisingly, this girl might've been just as easy as Yunyun.

"What about me?! Hey, Megumin, don't you have anything for me?! Give me a title I can brag about to people, too!"

This adult, who was sometimes more childlike than Iris, was the real problem.

As Cecily shook me by the shoulders to and fro, I said, "You are the manager of the Axis Church's Axel branch, aren't you? Don't you already have a good-enough title?"

"Not like that! I'd also like something more, you know, like right hand, or left hand, or girlfriend, or lover, or husband, or wife, or anything is fine. I just want an intimate role!"

"Some of those words don't go with the others! ...Well then, how about adviser? I'm sure you listen to confessions as a priestess anyway, so whenever we're in trouble, we can come to you for advice... Advice..."

Advice from her?

"Why can't you commit to your answer? Come to me for advice anytime you're in trouble! I'm especially good at romantic advice! I mean, you're going through puberty anyway, so it's perfect, right?"

Just when I was thinking how selfish an adult she was, Cecily suddenly said something intensely disturbing.

Sometimes this person was—how to put it?—scarily on point.

Struggling not to let on how startled I was, I said, "What are you talking about, Cecily? I am she who seeks to perfect the explosive path. I do not have a spare time to lose myself in something like love."

"That's right, Cecily—when Megumin starts talking about love, you'll wonder if a doppelgänger is impersonating her."

As Iris listened nervously to our conversation, Yunyun, who was clueless despite having been with me the longest, butted in with an unnecessary remark.

…Sometimes this girl was—how to put it?—dumb.

"Hmm. Recently, you seem vulnerable, or perhaps kinder or something… And once in a while, you get a look that makes me think, *This girl's in love.*"

I'd been looking down on her as an Axis follower, but maybe this lady wasn't just some weirdo.

"I was right; you have a love-like admiration for me, don't you?! You're a growing girl, after all; it can't be helped. As far as I'm concerned, you can bring it on! By the way, how about you be the husband four days a week and me three days a week? If I had to choose, I think you're better suited for the man's role."

It seemed my fear that Cecily was capable of understanding anything was unfounded.

With the words *talking about love* seeming to have grabbed her interest, Iris looked like she was itching to say something, but I wanted to avoid any further interrogation.

"Back to what I was saying! …We have now acquired a hideout and a source of income. Next, we'll recruit capable personnel. Right now, all we have are sideshows—pretty soon I'd like to get someone respectable."

"Wait just a minute there; I can't believe the biggest oddball among us said that. I guess I'm all for getting someone respectable soon, though. Like, someone I could go out to eat with, outside of meetings like these—someone nice…"

"An attacker, boss! Let's get an attacker adventurer so we can go on adventures!"

"According to my info," Cecily started, "there are four filthy-rich young men in this town. It would be perfect if they were blond upper-class hunks, but if they seem like they'll dote on me the rest of my life, I'm prepared to compromise."

Was it possible for the things they wanted to be any more different?

Kazuma's day-to-day leadership somehow started to seem really impressive.

"No, let's look for a Thief with good sense. We aren't here to recruit friends, adventuring companions, or husbands. Right now, we're all as far from being a thief gang as you can get."

"Eris followers call me a burglar sometimes, since I often snatch their supplies, so you could say I'm pretty well suited to a thief gang."

"You want to change jobs? I will take you to the Adventurers Guild and have you change classes for real, you know?"

It was at that moment…

"Speaking of blond upper-class hunks and personnel, have any of you heard? They say that in this town is a former nobleman of a neighboring country who now works as an adventurer."

…For some reason, Iris's eyes had lit up when she spoke.

Nobles generally had a lot of innate talent.

Maybe not as much as with royals like Iris, but they actively incorporated the genes of so-called heroes into their bloodlines by giving over their daughters as concubines.

"Former nobleman? I do not know why he is down on his luck, but he might have a bit of treasure hidden away. You have my attention."

Even Cecily appeared interested, though it was for a different reason than his potential or his talent.

"This is quite a famous story among the royals and nobles of various countries: A boy from the lower nobility in a neighboring nation received the super-rare title of Dragon Knight, and at the youngest age ever. Showing magnificent talent as a member of that class, the boy was the best spearman in the kingdom. Dragons had loved him since birth, too, and he was sincere, faithful, persevering, and good-natured, a shining example of a knight. Naturally, he was the target of the affections of many young women as well, but…

"It turned out that boy was appointed at a young age to be a bodyguard for a princess of that foreign country. No surprise that the princess, close in age, came to have feelings for him—anyone probably would've in that situation. However, the princess, being of royalty, already had a fiancé. Plus, she and the knight were of different social standings. The girl spent her days in joy and agony, unable to tell the boy her feelings. That boy, however, learned of her feelings by chance, and…

"…while knowing it would cause great trouble, the boy set the princess on the back of a dragon and whisked her away. Despite a countrywide search, no trace of them could be found, but about one week later, the boy returned to the castle, princess in tow, and although he avoided the death sentence, they stripped him of his right to be a Dragon Knight and of his inheritance."

The rest of us, who'd been hanging on every word, exhaled deeply after Iris's strangely moving story.

"In other words, he was a useless boy who kidnapped the princess and threw away the high life? Everyone knows kidnapping princesses is the job of evil wizards and the Demon King—you can't go taking another's job."

"N-no! This is the beautiful story of a romance forbidden by social class, and him trying to honor the feelings of the princess despite that! According to rumor, the princess was the one who asked him to let her ride on the dragon's back. I'm sure she said something like, *If only we could keep riding far away together…*while they were flying together!"

"Ooh! What is that? That's incredible! I-in other words, he threw away his honor as a national hero and then turned his back on a life of wealth so that he could grant the desire of the princess…?!"

Yunyun was unreasonably excited at hearing Iris's fantastical story.

"Yes, exactly! Even if he received punishment as a result, he fulfilled the dream she never thought would come true! That is the true account of things, according to the imaginations and rumors of noble and royal girls! What do you think? Isn't it dreamy and marvelous? It's a tragic love that's heartbreaking and sad…!"

I noticed she'd said it was a true story and then immediately proved it probably wasn't.

"In other words, Illis, you mean he's adventuring in exile? In this very town?! Let's get him to join! We definitely need him as our companion!"

The two of them were getting all excited, but it certainly would've been kinda cool if it was true.

Only if it was true, of course.

Maybe part of Iris sympathized with the princess in the story, being one herself.

And for Yunyun, too, having so few friends or companions, the thought of someone doing so much for another must have been moving.

"By the way, I wonder what happened during the week they were away? Could something big have happened that changed their lives? H-how far did they go…?!"

"What are you thinking about, Illis? Such a…! S-such a…!"

The two of them blushed as they squealed in excitement.

…It looked like the two young girls thought of the whole thing as a provocation for the imagination.

"I swear… Don't just sit there making noise—let us go find this person. Even I have experienced bathing and sleeping in the same bed as Kazuma. With our relationship the way it is, we will probably go all the way the moment the opportunity presents itself. That knight person must be older than us, so I'm sure he and the princess have crossed that line already."

"Hold on! I just heard Megumin say something very unsettling!"

"Me too!"

Both of them had previously been chattering to themselves on the sofa but now leaped to their feet.

"It's not unsettling; at our age, it's weirder not to have such experiences. Actually, in my case it's a matter of course, with us living under the same roof. Come on—let's go and find this champion. Calm down a bit more; look at Cecily—" While I spoke to the two girls who had their hands to their mouths in shock...

"Hey, Megumin, Cecily's asleep..."

"...It would be a pain if we woke her, so we shall let her sleep."

I reckoned I knew how Kazuma always felt looking after Aqua.

3

We walked through one of Axel's back alleys toward the Adventurers Guild.

The reason we didn't use the main paths was because the usual person was likely to come looking for Iris today, too.

Even if I thought that bodyguard wouldn't show her face today, it was definitely better to do everything possible not to stand out.

"So how are we supposed to find this ex–Dragon Knight elite-nobleman guy?" I asked Iris while appreciating the distinctive people-free feel of the alley.

"Right... They say he has blond hair, a long-standing trait of nobility. Since he was good enough to be the youngest Dragon Knight ever, he should stand out right away in this town. I guess another distinguishing feature would be that he was a master of the spear, even in his own country."

You didn't see many blond men around these parts. Even if you did, they were guaranteed to be connected to the nobility somehow. I was certain I had almost no memory of seeing any blond male adventurers, but...

"A-anyway, boss? A while back, when you said you'd bathed together with Kazuma and slept in the same bed..." Iris had been stuck on that point for a while now. Her voice was timid as she asked.

"I meant exactly what I said. Well, when a normal boy and girl have lived together for almost a year, it should not be that surprising."

"""!!"""

Ignoring both of them and their loss for words, I continued on with a smile of victory.

"Besides, as I said before, Kazuma and I have a promise to hang out in his room at some point, but going all the way so quickly would make him think I'm easy, you know. So, well, I've been putting it off as an adult's bargaining tactic..."

The forever-alone girl and the princess had looks of awe, but...

"W-well, you really just chickened out, though, didn't you? Or, like, something got in the way? When it comes to you, Megumin, I don't think such a thing would happen unless something spurred you on anyway. I bet you'd need the momentum from something really shocking to go through with it."

"Shut up! What would a total loner who's never even held a guy's hand know about it?!"

"?!"

Having brought Yunyun close to tears in an instant, I—an adult—took out the paper with my win-loss record against her and added a mark.

Watching out of the corner of her eye, Yunyun pretended to be calm, muttering, "Anyway, a skilled blond spearman who's also famous in this town...? Also, he must be well-mannered, sincere, faithful, and gentlemanly... Erm... A-and he must be tall and handsome...I hope..."

"You are mixing in your hopes there. Though lots of nobles are good-looking, and according to the story, he was a sincere individual, so I guess you are mostly right, but..."

Well, if he had so many distinguishing qualities, we'd surely find him in no time...

"I can't say I've heard of an adventurer with all those qualities."

I had been naive to even imagine finding such a legendary person was possible.

Arriving at the Adventurers Guild, we'd asked the receptionist lady right away, but...

"Is there anyone you can think of who might even be close? Not many adventurers use spears, and this town in particular has lots of problem-child adventurers, so I am sure he would stand out quite a bit based on his virtues alone."

"The adventurer party that stands out the most is yours, Miss Megumin. Though, even if there were some folks who fit one or two parts of that description, I can't think of anyone who matches all of them..."

We turned to each other at the troubled-looking woman's disappointing words.

"...Well then, could you please introduce us to those you said matched some of the traits?"

Thus.

The receptionist directed us to the partially matching candidates so that our search for the Dragon Knight, famed abroad in years past, could continue...

"...In my life up till now, I don't recall ever being inferior to anyone, and I'm confident I've lived faithfully. I am also assured in my skills and I used to be well-known enough... Do you have some sort of business with a retired guy like me?"

The first person she introduced us to was an old man.

"Erm, I thought perhaps I'd like to listen to your tales. Okay, Illis and Yunyun, it's your turn. Illis, you look up to adventurers, so you must like their stories, right? And you can talk with him all you want, Yunyun. You're happy to get to talk with a new friend, aren't you?"

"Please do tell me about your adventures when you were young, sir!"

"Huh?! I'm very happy just to get to talk with someone, but isn't he totally the wrong age to be the one we're looking for?!"

For now, I thrust the sincere-seeming old man we were introduced to on the two of them.

*   *   *

"…Indeed, I am famous enough and on the competent side, but I've never touched a spear. Well actually, I do touch another sort of spear every night! Know what I mean? *Gah-ha-ha-ha-ha!*"

The next adventurer we were introduced to, despite just meeting us, suddenly busted out a terrible dirty joke and got his face acquainted with my fist.

"…Indeed, the spear is a great specialty of mine, and not a competitor out there doesn't know my name, but… Still, this is quite rare, for girls to take an interest in a sport like spear throwing."

That Guild lady set me up with someone who wasn't even a real adventurer.

A little later…

"Oh? What're you doing here? Aren't you that Explosion girl? What business could you possibly have with me? If it's about money, I can't help you—nobody's gonna lend me any more anyway. I don't even have enough for booze. Actually, could you lend me some? If I ever happen to hit it rich, I'll give you back double."

The person she introduced as the last one meeting my conditions was this blond-haired punk named Dust.

Dust was a man who, instead of working, lazed about in a corner of the Adventurers Guild complaining about not having any cash.

I forcefully pulled away the receptionist lady who'd introduced me to such a person.

"Excuse me, that there is definitely not him. We are searching for a young, blond, handsome, skilled, reasonably famous, sincere, faithful, persevering, and gentlemanly spearman. That guy there only matches the blond part. Even then, he's a dirty blond at best."

"If someone as dreamy as that existed, I'd be the one wanting an introduction… There are no other adventurers I know who even come close to matching all those qualities. The only blond adventurers in Axel are Miss Lalatina and Mr. Dust anyway… He may always be dead drunk, but at least he is surprisingly skilled and famous…"

"By 'famous,' you must mean infamous! I saw you tell new adventurers not to go near him!"

The people before him had been bad enough, but Dust felt like I'd been forced to draw the shortest straw.

"Come ooon! We're buddies, Yunyun; at least buy me some booze!"

"You're just an acquaintance, not a friend! The people around us are gonna look down on me even more than they already do, so stop it!"

At some point while I was talking to the receptionist lady, Dust had gotten ahold of Yunyun.

With my hand, I signaled for Iris, who was still listening to the old man's stories of adventure, and said, "Illis, listen. The receptionist says the only blond male adventurer in town is that guy over there."

"The old man was just getting to a good part. There was a One-Punch Bear that broke his spear, and he awoke to the power of his bare hands and made up his mind to fight with everything he had… If that man over there is the only one, then why don't we go listen to what he has to say?"

Iris seemed disappointed at first, but she suggested we feel out things with Dust.

"No, I can say for sure that guy is definitely not the knight. If we let our eyes off him for a second, that guy will go get Kazuma into trouble—he's what you would call 'bad company,'" I explained, watching said punk as he continued to bother Yunyun.

That said, Yunyun was being unusually assertive in her protests. She was usually so quiet. What could have happened between the two of them?

Lately I'd been hearing rumors that she had been hanging around some odd folks, so could that have had something to do with this guy?

Up until now, I hadn't paid much attention to her, but maybe it would've been better to look after her. I didn't want any weirdos getting ahold of her.

"Oh, I know that guy. He was the one who bumped into a woman passing by and then claimed to have a broken leg, or whatever, on this one trip I took into town. He was trying to intimidate that lady by saying, 'Buy me a meal as compensation.' I remember sending Claire after him as punishment…"

Seriously, what was Dust doing?

Seeming to have finally thrown away even his pride, Dust was bowing down at Yunyun's feet, probably begging for money so he could drink.

Looking embarrassed, Yunyun was getting some cash out of her wallet in a flustered panic. Bowing down in public to get someone to buy something seemed like a form of intimidation in and of itself.

A former Dragon Knight who squeezed beer money from younger girls and bowed down in public…

"…Yep, there is no way it is him. So that means the knight must have gone to some other town. There is not much we can do if we do not even have his name. How about we give up for the day and hang at the hideout before going home?"

"Boss, I feel like intelligence gathering in times like these is exactly what thieves do. Can we really call ourselves a thief gang…?"

Iris hit me where it hurt, but this was no time to be talking about that…

…*Hmm?*

"Illis, you just made a really good point! That's right—we're a bandit crew. What we should be searching for is a talented Thief!"

"I-it seems a bit late for that. For a wizard like you to be saying such things as the boss of a thief gang is—"

"Hush, that's not important right now! I just found someone who looks like a Thief, right when we need them! Come on, Illis! Let us go!"

Taking the confused Iris along, I ran over to someone I hadn't seen come by the Guild in a long time.

4

"Nice to see you. It has been a while, Chris. I know this is sudden, but we have formed a thief gang, so please join."

"*Pfft!*"

As I extended my invitation immediately following my greeting, Chris gloriously spat out the milk she had been drinking.

"What are you doing? A young woman should not be spitting out milk in a public place."

"*Cough, cough*... Don't ask me what I'm doing! You know it's because you opened with something so ridiculous all of a sudden!"

I hadn't seen Chris since the Eris Appreciation Festival, but here she was, taking a break by herself. She wore a satisfied look, as though the Thief had just completed a job.

Seeing that, I tried talking to her, of course, but...

"You say it's ridiculous, but seeing as you're a Thief, it wouldn't be that odd if you were part of a crew of bandits, would it?"

"Y-y-y-yeah, but! Yeah, but! I mean, what does that even mean?! Listen, you aren't trying to tease me because you know who I really am, are you, Megumin?!"

As I stood perplexed about the odd thing Chris had said, Iris caught up. I briefly explained my relationship with Chris to the princess.

Curiously, despite it being their first meeting, Iris cocked her head to the side.

"Er, is your name Chris? I beg your pardon, but haven't we met somewhere?"

At the sudden question, the Thief also cocked her head...

"Your name is Illis, right? A second ago, I thought I'd seen you before, too...er, ahhh?!"

It seemed like she recognized Iris as a royal. Right, all she really did to conceal herself was use the dubious name Illis. Most of the time she didn't even hide her face.

There were probably pictures of royals' faces floating all over the place.

"Just as I would expect from a well-informed Thief, you seem to know who Illis really is, but she is incognito. It would be a problem if we caused a commotion, so could you...?" I thought she was surprised to realize Illis was a royal, but something was odd about Chris's manner.

"I—I see! Well, I am a Thief, you know?! When you're like me, you know who someone is and where they're from at first glance! If she's incognito, then it can't be helped. W-well then, I have some errands to run, so I'll be off—"

She said something that made no sense and tried to leave, but I promptly grabbed her.

"Where are you going? Since you're so well-informed, I have something to ask of you."

"Wh-what might that be? I'm a pure and upstanding Thief for justice with nothing on my conscience, but I don't think there's anything I could help you with."

Then, as I held on to her arm, she glanced suspiciously back at Iris.

"I'm not exactly trying to do anything to you. Like I said a second ago, we made a crew for thievery, but we're having trouble finding some real talent. We were able to get a ton of Knights, Arch-wizards, and Priests, but despite calling it a thief gang, we don't have a single all-important, actual Thief..."

"You can get Knights, Arch-wizards, and Priests? Hey, wouldn't you make more money just dropping the whole gang thing and being a mercenary band or something? It seems like you've already succeeded at gathering together a much more exclusive group..."

As Chris looked to be thinking hard, sure enough, Iris seemed doubtful.

"I cannot complain about their fighting ability, of course. But since we require an actual Thief, I want to ask you to join, Chris. Also, we are actually looking for another person as well. I would also like to ask you to help search for them."

"A thief gang, huh...? I mean, I got myself involved in a few things after admiring a similar kind of group. So I do understand how you feel, you know?"

It was a better response than I had expected.

"You really do understand. Actually, we also formed this group because we admired a certain group of famous bandits... By the way, do you know the so-called Silver-Haired Thief Brigade?"

"Yeah, I know them. I guess I probably know them a lot better than anyone else does."

Of course! Chris was part of an intelligence network—as expected of a true-blue Thief.

I bent down and lowered my voice. "Actually, this is just between us, but all of us admire the Silver-Haired Thief Brigade. Influenced by their actions, we are trying to support them secretly from the shadows, giving those heroes what little assistance we can. They know nothing about our activities. You might call it an evolved fan club."

"I seeee… Hey, Megumin, just asking, but you're not making fun of me, are you?"

For some reason, Chris had a far-off look, as if she knew way more than I ever could.

"What are you talking about? We are serious! Ahhh, did supporting criminals with a bounty on their heads sound like I was kidding? Just between us, there is actually a reason they have a bounty on them."

"Ahhh, yeah. I know about that, too, so don't worry. So basically, I guess you're like an unofficial subsidiary supporting the Silver-Haired Thief Brigade? And you want me to join, you say."

"That is correct. Please join, even as a provisional member, if you prefer. Of course, in that case, you would be considered the grunt in the beginning."

At that, Chris made an interesting face with a mixture of uncertainty and suspicion.

"G-grunt… I'll be the grunt of a Silver-Haired Thief Brigade subsidiary…? I mean, well, I don't mind going along with it, you know? Anyway, Megumin, I know I keep asking, but you're not yanking my chain, already knowing everything, are you?"

"…Why have you been so paranoid all this time?"

"I'm supposed to have good luck, right? Why do I keep ending up in such amusing situations…? Like during the Eris Appreciation Festival, when, for some reason, I had to help out at the Axis Church's stall. Or…I guess like right now, too…"

5

I told Chris, who ended up going with the flow and joining us, about the matter of the Dragon Knight.

"If the ex–Dragon Knight has blond hair, isn't that him over there?" she asked, pointing to, of course, Dust.

Over there, perhaps unwilling to let Yunyun go after just a single cup of booze, he had begun some kind of lecture about human relations.

I thought even Yunyun would try to give him a beating for preaching about getting along with people, but she was nodding interestedly with a *hmm-hmm* and taking notes.

"That is not him. I guess there are things even someone as well-informed as you does not know."

"Huh?! B-but the person you're looking for is blond, right? I'm pretty sure the only adventurers with blond hair in this town are him and Darkness."

This was already old news to me.

"Blond hair is the only thing that punk has in common with the person I am looking for. I swear, how blind are you, Chris?"

"A-am I?! I'm pretty sure you're the one person I don't wanna hear that from in this situation, Megumin!"

I was about to ask what she meant by that, but suddenly I noticed something.

"…I was thinking, you have been awfully quiet for a little while now; what is wrong?"

"No, I just have a feeling I really have met Chris before, but I can't remember where…"

"You don't need to remember! I have no memory of meeting you to begin with, Illis, so I'm sure this is the first time!"

Chris is getting awfully flustered.

"Anyway, about that person you said you're looking for. My intuition tells me it's definitely that blond guy over there. He's wearing a sword, but his footwork and the casual way he maintains spacing seem like that of a spear user. And by my reckoning, he looks like quite an expert."

Chris's face turned suddenly serious as she cast a glance at Dust, who had now stood up in front of Yunyun and was busy doing something bizarre.

"Take a good look—people won't make light of you if you walk like this. You're so desperate for friends, you try to lick the boots of others. When people look down on you as an adventurer, it's over. Just like dogs and cats, first impressions decide who's superior!"

As we watched, Dust squared his shoulders and started moving unsteadily, like a drunkard, swaying his body around. As onlookers stared inquisitively, thinking Yunyun and the drunk were buddies, the forever-alone girl cringed in embarrassment.

"…I see. So that is an expert spearman's footwork. You have quite the observant eye, Chris."

"Why did that guy have to start doing something weird right when I said something?!"

…Continuing to garner the attention of onlookers for some time afterward with his bizarre movements, Dust left the Guild with Yunyun, as if it was the most everyday thing in the world.

Yunyun kept looking our way like she wanted help, but given Chris had said this was the guy we were looking for, we ended up letting her go along with Dust so we could tail them.

When I signaled for her to go with it, Yunyun followed along in resignation.

"If you are so adamant about it, then I am willing to use her as a sacrifice, but I do not think that is him."

"My gut tells me he's putting on an act. There must be some reason he pretends to be an idiot."

I had no idea why she wanted him to be a secret expert so bad, but Chris seemed to recognize Dust as quite the pro, in her mind, at least.

My gut told me this wasn't her pretending but straight-up bona fide idiocy.

After all, when he came to my house the other day to ask Kazuma to hang out, he had a straight-faced, lively, and sacrilegious discussion with Aqua, who was loafing around at home, about why so many Eris followers had small boobs.

We followed for a bit…

"His gait seems a bit awkward to me, too. Like he's trying to force a new way of moving after abandoning what was deeply ingrained for many years… Actually, I kind of feel an aura of strength coming from that person."

It would've been one thing if it was just Chris, but now Iris, a powerful combatant in her own right, had praised Dust.

Surely that guy couldn't really be…?

Ahead of us, on the other hand, Yunyun opened her mouth to say something while Dust was taking her who-knows-where.

"Aren't you walking a bit funny today, Dust? You seem to be limping. Is your leg hurt…?"

"Oh, you can tell? Nah, it's just a little pain; I'm not injured or anything. The other day, I heard from my buddy Keith about, uhhh, what would you call it? He told me about a way to make a you-know-what get bigger even after you've stopped growing, so I tried it out. Of course, it involved using minced ginger, raw garlic, and wasabi… Hey, why are you looking at me like that? That wasn't a come-on this time, so stop chanting that spell."

Even after saying something so vulgar to such a young girl, Dust continued.

"Look, girls try drinking milk and massaging and whatnot to make their boobs bigger, right? Every boy has the dream of making his you-know-what bigger. You have things you want, too, don't you? You dream of having friends, and I dream of being huge. Aren't both our goals marvelous?"

…A young girl's longtime, earnest dream of having friends and a guy's dream of being a big guy.

I watched Yunyun start arguing with Dust, yelling at him not to ruin her childhood dream.

"You two have some incredible judgment. Apparently, *that's* the reason for that awkward walk of his."

Chris and Iris, who had been explaining things to me with such confidence, hid their red faces.

6

"Hey, Yunyun got mad and went home—is there still any point in tailing him? Shadowing a guy like this makes me feel like I have really hit rock bottom." With her pure childhood dream now categorized with the vilest one, Yunyun left.

We continued on with our shadowing. Chris, now acting partly out of obstinance, led the group.

"My gut tells me there's definitely something about him. I have a better eye for people than my looks would suggest. I can see through to the real him... At least, I think so. I'm not in the zone right now, so I can't be absolutely sure."

I wasn't quite sure what she meant by "in the zone," but for how good her eye for people was supposed to be, I seemed to recall her not worrying about Vanir and Wiz when she'd seen them at the Eris Appreciation Festival, despite being a zealous follower of Eris herself.

"I just have one thing to ask: What do you think of the undead and devils, Chris?"

"I think they should all burn in Hell."

That was fast.

"Even if it was a person who had no choice but to become an undead to fulfill some heartfelt wish, or if it was a devil who basically loved teasing people but didn't seem as bad as you thought once you got to know them...?"

"I think they should all burn, without any exceptions."

A typical Eris follower.

This was what it meant to give no quarter.

She probably didn't think of Vanir as anything more than a bit of a weirdo, either, but this really showed me how blind Chris was.

Then, as Chris looked perplexed at my sudden question...

"Ah, both of you, over there!"

When we looked where Iris was pointing, we saw Dust making sure nobody was around as he stood in front of a trash heap that crows had strewn about.

"Huh, he really is an honest person after all. Look, look, he's doing good deeds when nobody's around to notice. After he's gone out of his way to make sure no one is around, he's gonna start cleaning up the garbage. Even regular people don't usually do that. He's looking more and more like the person you're searching for!"

...Not exactly.

"I see, so he's sifting through the unsorted trash. I really had this individual misjudged! He must have had some noble reason when he hassled that lady on the street before, too...!"

Both of them were gloriously mistaken—he was going through the refuse to search for anything he could sell.

As proof, when he found something that seemed worth selling, he rejoiced with a huge smile plastered on his face.

"See, Megumin, my eyes aren't so bad, huh?"

She was just as blind as Aqua.

"Look at that! He's not just sorting the trash but even cleaning up what was scattered around. The ex–Dragon Knight in the story was said to have a sincere, faithful, and persevering personality, after all..."

Not knowing much about garbage, Iris seemed to have a strange misunderstanding—clearly, he was doing it because leaving the refuse scattered would make it difficult for him to go through it later on.

Having found something of value, Dust was beside himself as he cleaned up the trash heap and took what he found straight to the nearby hardware shop.

"He found that a moment ago, right? Is it okay to exchange something you found for money, even if it was in a pile of garbage?"

Chris volunteered to answer Iris and her doubts.

"W-well, it was thrown out, after all. Rather than leaving it thrown away, I guess reusing it like that would be better for the world…"

Ignoring what both of them said…

"It seems that perhaps he did not agree with the buying price, because it looks like he just started arguing… Ah, I guess they ended up winning, since now he is venting frustration by kicking the garbage bin out all over the ground!"

"""……"""

The two of them, who'd been looking smug as they praised Dust, once again covered their red faces.

…We continued to follow him thereafter.

"Look, Megumin, over there—he's helping a woman who's being hassled by some foreign adventurer! He's gonna do a good deed this time for sure…!"

"…He's started bothering her himself now, demanding she date him as thanks."

He ran away once the police warned him to stop harassing her.

"…Oh, Dust dropped his wallet."

"He sure did. This isn't the time for stalking; we have to pick it up and return it… Oh, the person walking behind him is returning it. That's good!"

"Wait, oh no! He's arguing now, something like, *I'm sure I had more in my wallet. You stole it, didn't you?!*"

Having deliberately dropped his wallet and argued with the young man who picked it up for him, Dust bolted again after the police showed up.

"This is our chance! A newbie adventurer is practicing his spear play in an empty lot! If Dust is a spear master, I'm sure he'll do something…!"

"…He went by, picking his nose, showing no interest whatsoever."

"...In fact, he's making a fuss to the police who came after him earlier. Looks like he's asking why they don't scold an adventurer who's waving a weapon around in town."

It was thus that Dust relentlessly showed us his pathetic stripes.

After fully and shamelessly demonstrating that he was the loser to be most wary of in this town, he finally...

"...Then I boldly leaped out in front of the Kowloon Hydra as a decoy to protect the other adventurers from danger. I was sent to Lady Eris when it killed me. Man, seeing her with my own eyes... Dang, she was divine."

"Ooh...! I want to meet Lady Eris, too, but that won't happen when I die of old age. I'm sure going somewhere dangerous and throwing away one's life on purpose would go against her will, too. I'm so jealous you got to meet her...!"

Having made an utter nuisance of himself as he wandered around town, Dust returned to the Adventurers Guild and was now telling fishy tales to an old Eris priest he'd grabbed.

As I recalled, the souls of people who met an unlucky fate, like getting killed by monsters, did make their way to the goddess Eris. Things like death from old age were not included in that, of course.

It wasn't completely unbelievable that, if Dust did die from a Kowloon Hydra, he would have met the goddess, but...

"And so Lady Eris says to me, 'You are not meant to die here. You are destined to aid the hero who will defeat the Demon King someday. Come now—return to us and help the hero who will save this world. I pray that you may bring light upon the land...'"

"Wow, Lady Eris said that?! You sure carry a great destiny on your shoulders! If there is anything I can do to help, don't hesitate to ask!"

It was rather dubious whether Eris really told him that. For some reason, Chris started to tremble when she saw the priest so sincerely moved.

As a devout follower of Eris herself, perhaps Chris was jealous that Dust had met her.

His tale concluded, Dust chugged a drink the clergyman had

bought as thanks for the story. The blond man turned with a smile toward the naive-seeming priest...

"Oh, really? Actually, I'd love to fight alongside the hero and save the world, but sadly, I don't have the money... I wonder if there are any devout followers of Eris around who'd be my patron, for the sake of world peace..."

"What did you saaaaaaay?!"

Chris grabbed ahold of Dust.

7

"Come on—what're you doing? I was this close. Ah, you're that girl, right? The Thief who Kazuma yanked the panties off of when you two first met. Didn't you run away crying after that?"

"I—I—I didn't cry! Anyway, that was an accident!"

We treated Dust to a meal at a table in one corner of the Adventurers Guild.

When Chris had suddenly flown into a rage and grabbed the man, he'd complained that she was interfering with business. Somehow, the tables had turned, and the Thief was buying him food after he got angry...

"Boss, is it true that Kazuma stripped off Chris's panties? You said earlier you were bathing with him, too. What is he getting up to?"

"That sort of thing is business as usual for him. Just the other day at the mansion, he was trying to pull down Darkness's underwear in the bathroom stall."

"What could possibly lead to a situation like that?!"

As I was filling Iris in on all of Kazuma's sexual harassment, Dust went wild ordering everything he could on Chris's dime, saying, "Speaking of, I guess you were all tailing me today; what was that about? Are you guys my fans?"

"No one would be weird enough to be your fan... Er, wait, you noticed us? I didn't use my Ambush skill, but still—just as I thought, you're more than just some nobody, aren't you?" Chris asked suggestively, still seemingly unable to let go of the idea of Dust being a former noble elite.

"Nah, you all stand out like crazy. I'm sure anyone would've noticed with that loud fuss you were making."

"W-well, whatever. Anyway, you—just because you met Eris doesn't mean you can spread lies, you know! Don't come crying to me when she smites you!"

It was hard to believe such a levelheaded Thief was this devout a follower of Eris.

Unperturbed by Chris's anger, Dust said, "Hey, hey, how would you know if I was lying? You've never met Lady Eris, right? That's right, you haven't; you can't meet her unless you die, after all."

"Well... I—I mean, Lady Eris would never say something so prophetic..." Chris averted her eyes awkwardly, sensing her weakened position.

Seemingly unable to repress her curiosity, Iris leaned in. "What sort of individual was Lady Eris? Did she look just like she does in the pictures?"

"Oh, who's this? I haven't seen your face around. Lady Eris was just as front-heavy as the Axis Church claims her to be, which was obviously because of pad— Er, aaahhhh!"

After his sacrilegious remark, Dust got a better look at Iris's face and let out a shriek.

"Wait a second! You can't go around spreading that talk about pads!"

"Shut up! Who cares about a goddess's boob pads right now?! Hey, kid, aren't you that brat who was with Vanir's master and set your short-tempered blond bodyguard on me while I was hitting on chicks?! That scary suit lady isn't here today, is she?!"

"Ummm, if you mean Claire, she isn't here right now."

Now that he mentioned it, I did seem to remember Iris saying something like that a while back.

"Wait, you seriously have to stop mentioning boob pads! Anyway, you can't make up conversations with Lady Eris—she really will smite you, okay?!"

Dust grinned amusedly at Chris as she slammed the table with a *wham*.

"Like I said, do you have any proof I lied? I tell you, even though it was the first time we met, Lady Eris was obviously into me. The look she had was unmistakable."

"No, she was looking at you with pity, like anyone would look after someone died in such a stupid way!"

"Don't insult me like that, as if you were there yourself! I bravely charged the Kowloon Hydra—now apologize!"

"All you did was lose your mind trying to get all the glory for yourself!"

Their argument didn't look like it was going to calm down, but once Dust's food arrived, they seemed to call a temporary truce.

"...Well? Getting back on topic, why were you following me?"

"As it happens, I recently formed a thief gang with a certain goal in mind. Then I heard rumors about a blond and handsome expert adventurer, so I decided to recruit him. When I asked the receptionist lady if such a person existed, she told me you were the only adventurer with the right color of hair, so I figured I'd measure your ability..."

His face stuffed full of food, Dust swallowed and impolitely pointed his fork my way.

"A handsome expert adventurer? I swear, all anyone cares about these days is looks. I'll let Kazuma know later that you were all trying to pick up hot adventurers."

"N-no, we were not trying to pick up anyone! Besides, I personally do not care if they're not hot; that is just what the rumor said!"

For some reason, I stammered an excuse. Dust gazed my way, doubtful.

"What sort of person is this guy you're looking for? I guess this panties-stripped girl couldn't find him, but I know a lot about this town's adventurers, even if I don't look it. Anyone can dye their hair, after all. Try me: What's this guy like?"

"He was supposed to be a blond, handsome, highly skilled, sincere, faithful, persevering individual. Supposedly, all the young women idolized him."

"......Does anyone like that really exist in this world?" Dust asked, looking more and more unsure. "If we're talking someone similar to that, I guess there's just that weirdo named Mitsu...something-or-other. Was he really that stalwart, though? He got super mad when I touched the butt of the chick he was with."

It was glaringly obvious we really had asked the wrong person.

"Er, do you mind if I ask you something?" Iris spoke up after having remained silent for a while.

"Huh? What is it, kiddo? I don't have a girlfriend or anything, but unlike Kazuma, I'm not a loli-lover, got it?"

"Please don't call him a 'loli-lover'! No, that's not it... Er, do you ever use a spear?"

His eyebrow perking up at the mention of a spear, Dust scratched his head a bit awkwardly.

"I—"

"Lady Illiiiiiiiiiiiis!"

No sooner had Dust started than he was cut off by a yell echoing throughout the Guild Hall.

The owner of the voice was none other than Claire, Iris's bodyguard.

"Ahhh! You're that weird chick who took swipes at me out of nowhere before!"

"Ahhh! You're that skirt-chasing wretch from before! I won't let you get your claws on Lady Illis this time...!"

"Liar! Hey, kiddo, didn't you say this chick wasn't around today?!"

"Th-there was no way I could..."

Dust, frightened by the woman in the white suit, fled the scene, his complaint to Iris trailing off behind him.

...Chris and I saw the princess off. After, we realized how late it was and decided to call it a day.

"No fabled ex–Dragon Knight after all. Well, I am glad you joined up at least, Chris."

"That adds up. No expert adventurer would have a reason to stay in a beginners' town. But anyway, I guess that Dust guy wasn't him. I was sure I had an eye for people, though..."

Vanir and Wiz standing out as much as they did was proof this girl was as blind as a bat.

"But why did that Dragon Knight make off with the princess? The story may have been lovely as Illis told it, but he must have had his reasons."

"Well, everyone has a secret or two. I myself have something I have never shown anyone, not even Kazuma."

We Crimson Magic Clansfolk were each born with a number and mark on different spots of our bodies.

In my case, it was sort of on a spot I couldn't show other people...

"Megumin, a girl shouldn't say they'll show that to just anyone, you know?"

"I am not necessarily talking about anything lewd! Anyway, you have at least one secret of your own, don't you, Chris?!"

The Thief giggled quietly at that.

"I guess I might have a few I keep from you, Megumin—secrets I share with Kazuma, at that."

"Oh, are you challenging me? That is a challenge, right? Fine, I am sick of seeing all the hussies ogling him recently—bring it on!"

"W-w-w-wait a sec, I'm not like that!"

8

Cecily was still sleeping like a log when we got back to the hideout, so I decided to head home.

The priestess was so totally smitten with the place, it seemed she would live there in a heartbeat. It was probably better to have someone always there than to leave it empty anyway.

Today, we got a really good new member. Yes, the Thief we'd been waiting so long for, at last.

Somehow, we'd been straying off course at every turn, but now we could finally get down to some real banditry.

It was like, everyone was so unique, it made it hard to keep everyone on track.

Kazuma might have actually been a genius to get such people to do what he wanted and to bring them together when it counted.

…Pondering leadership qualities on my way back to the mansion, a familiar figure caught my eye.

It was the newbie adventurer who had been practicing his spear play in an empty lot. He was still swinging his spear around, despite the setting sun. Dust watched him quietly from a short distance. He was probably just going to mess with the newbie again. Checking for police nearby, the blond man approached the newbie adventurer.

"…Hey, lemme see that spear a sec. I'll show you how it's done," he said rather unexpectedly.

The adventurer, perhaps ignorant of Dust's notoriety, wiped sweat from his brow and handed over the spear.

Checking its length and condition, Dust swung the spear around for the while with a *whoosh*, and then he showed off some thrusts. Even to an amateur like me, it looked well practiced. The newbie adventurer stopped wiping himself off, his gaping mouth confirming the same thing I was seeing. The sound of the spear slicing through the air became sharper with each swing. The newbie was totally stunned.

A growing sense of tension gripped me.

Dust oozed such concentration that it made me wonder where the usual loser had gone; finally, he came to a low squat with the spear held at the ready, and…

"…I'm home!"

"Welcome back. Tonight's dinner is everyone's favorite, beef hot pot. I'm sick of Aqua saying, 'Come on, come on,' so go ahead and wash up." Kazuma was today's chef. He was carrying a gently boiling pot.

Aqua was already seated at the table, and Darkness, who'd apparently been waiting on me, was pouring booze for everyone.

"Kazuma, I have a little something to ask—do you mind?"

"Oh, what's this all of a sudden? …Ahaaa, you wanna ask when

I'm going to bed?" he said with feigned ignorance, apparently thinking about our promise the other day.

"No, not that. It is… Do you have anything you're keeping from someone else? Like a secret, or something like that."

"A secret? I have tons of secrets. I mean, who doesn't?"

…I guess that's true.

The spectacle I'd witnessed just before was so shocking, it'd made me ask something silly. Could Dust really have been that Dragon Knight? His last technique had been almost unbelievable.

If he hadn't brought me back down to reality by saying, *"Bring me one million eris if you want me to teach you that,"* I might've been overwhelmed.

"What are you on about so suddenly, Megumin? By the way, I don't have any secrets. I trust all of you. I've told you everything there is about me." Darkness spoke to me with a soft smile as I contemplated.

"Funny you'd say that, since you joined the party pretending not to be a girl and caused that big scene when you tried to get married in secret."

Suddenly, Darkness looked ready to cry as Kazuma instantly won the argument.

Then Aqua, who was excitedly waiting for the hot pot meat to cook, said, "Oh my, even I have secrets, you know? Actually, I was thinking I should let everyone know soon."

"Come on! You're just gonna tell everyone you're a goddess again, right? I told you, you're never gonna get these two to believe you…"

"No, not that. It's coming up on a year since we formed our party, and I couldn't help drinking the expensive booze Kazuma bought to celebrate!"

Kazuma suddenly froze at Aqua's words.

"My bad!"

"Whaddaya mean, 'My bad'? You bonehead! That's called dishonesty, not a secret! …Hey, those are some shifty eyes there. You were probing to see if I'd get mad about something petty because you have a bigger secret to hide, don't you?! Come on—tell me!"

...Oh well.

Even I was still keeping the thief gang's presence hidden from Kazuma.

I just ignored the two of them. They were busy arguing like they always did anyway...

Tilting a wineglass, Darkness asked me cheerfully, "By the way, Megumin, apparently you've been spending time with a lot of different people recently? What on earth were you doing today?"

Huh. What had happened today? A bunch of stuff, I guess? I got another grunt, but if I had to pick something...

"I saw some surprisingly different sides to a few different people today. If they give the okay, I will tell you about it sometime. I am sure you will be shocked."

This was like Iris or Yunyun, but I'd definitely have to ask what had really happened with the princess next time.

Chapter
4

The
Thief
Gang
Raids

1

At the hideout, which had completely transformed into just a place to hang out...

Chris suddenly spoke up while looking over the list of applicants for my thief gang.

"I just don't get it."

To the Thief who stared dumbfounded and motionless at the list, I said, "What are you on about all of a sudden? I do not get what is difficult to understand. That is the list of people wanting to join my crew."

"How are there so many?! Plus, how did you manage to get the best mansion in Axel as your hideout, and why does the list include the names of famous experts?!"

Just what was wrong with this grunt?

"What are you making such a fuss about? It's a good thing for an organization to be big."

"It is, but— Wait, is it?! Hey, does Kazuma know about this?!" asked my underling with a confused look on her face.

"I have told him I got new companions and a hideout, stuff like that."

"I—I see. So he still doesn't really know everything... Huh? Am I the only one who thinks this is pretty important?"

It seemed Chris was a worrywart—she was a grunt, after all.

"Are you surprised at the scale of it? Well, this is what happens when I am in charge."

"Huuuuh...? Y-you're pretty good, Megumin..." Chris looked at me with a mixture of surprise and awe.

But then...

"Don't talk like you weren't worried about it getting bigger than you expected," Yunyun muttered quietly while expertly constructing a house of cards on the table.

"Hey, if you do not want all your hard work this morning to be destroyed, you ought to watch your mouth."

"F-fine. I'm going to break my record with five decks of cards today, so cut it out."

At some point, Yunyun had gotten good at playing alone—what exactly was this girl's goal?

"By the way...," Chris said somewhat awkwardly. "Who's that person who keeps staring at me over there?" The Thief glanced at Cecily, who was peeking her head out from behind the sofa. Despite being a huge fan of girls, Cecily was strangely on her guard around Chris for some reason.

"That's Cecily, a priestess who's made herself at home here... What's wrong, Cecily? You're always acting crazy, but you're being especially strange today."

The clergywoman eyed Chris suspiciously while I asked her what was the matter.

"I'm not really sure myself, but my pretty-little-girl sensors aren't responding. This is the first time that's happened, so I'm not sure what to do... Excuse me, might you be a boy pretending to be a little girl? Actually, I wouldn't mind that, so something's gotta be wrong."

"People sometimes mistake me for a boy when I wear shorts, but I'm as female as they come..."

Chris seemed somewhat crestfallen, apparently having been mistaken for a boy before thanks to her short hair and rough garb.

"Ahhh, Chris is a devout follower of Eris. Maybe that is why you two are not compatible."

Hearing the words "follower of Eris," Cecily stood up from where she hid behind the sofa.

"What?! I can't allow a follower of Eris to intrude on my sanctuary of pretty little girls! ...Aha, you're here because you wanted to steal my life of lazing around with young cuties to dote on me every day? You think I'm gonna let you take away such a lovely position, you thieving cat?!"

"'Thieving cat'?! H-hold on a sec. There seems to be a weird misunderstanding—I was practically half forced to join...!"

Cecily, seemingly allergic to Eris followers, lashed out at Chris...

"Speaking of, Yunyun, is Illis not here today?"

"When I went to the usual meeting spot, her maid gave me a message that she couldn't come because of a ceremony or something... C-cut it out—don't blow on the cards like that. Megumin, I'm about to go crazy wondering who that girl really is..."

A royal event, huh?

We'd finally gotten enough people, so I'd been thinking about conducting a raid soon, but oh well.

"That sort of thing cannot be helped, I suppose. It sure would be a problem trying to drag her here if there is a ceremony to attend."

"Hey, Megumin, who is Illi—? Why are you averting your eyes? Why are you looking away, too, Chris?! Wait, don't shake me; my tower's gonna fall!"

After I shook Yunyun by the shoulders to shut her up, I said, "And so now that we have a professional Thief, I would like to finally conduct a raid! It shall be on the first day Illis can participate! Until then, I shall research the raid target and formulate a plan... That is all!" I pounded the table with my fist to show how serious my declaration was...

"Ahhhh, my tower! Waaaiiit!"

…That night.

Having finished supper back home, I approached Kazuma with something to ask.

"The secret to managing problem children? What an odd thing to ask out of the blue."

I'd tried planning a raid, but the characters I'd recruited made for a thief gang full of easily distracted people.

I wanted to learn the secret to managing troublesome companions from Kazuma, who had an established reputation for doing just that.

I had asked him that very thing, but…

"There's no secret or anything. I'm not really even trying to manage anyone. Even monster tamers can't give really specific orders to the monsters they keep. I'm just winging it, guiding all of you with vague instructions."

"'Vague instructions,' huh? You do a good job dealing with it all."

Though, now that he mentioned it, Kazuma didn't exactly give such specific directions each time.

"I mean, even if I gave you specific directions, none of you would listen. A top online gamer like me can wing it by judging the situation as it unfolds. In the guild I was in back in my home country, there were lots of problem children worse than all of you."

"'Top' meaning you were high on the leaderboards, right? So you had brothers-in-arms—you did say you attacked forts and hunted bosses together."

That was one of the many mysteries surrounding Kazuma. He'd said he'd hunted monsters and bosses with his comrades for days at a time, all through the night, making a decent-enough name for himself.

"Yeah, I was considered one of the central guild members, you know. I was in charge of training newbs and scheduling fights against tough enemies. I think that helped prepare me to deal with people like you all." Kazuma's words were brimming with unerring confidence.

He'd spoken about this before, and I was convinced he wasn't lying.

"I guess if I had to say there was any sort of trick to it, it's trying to understand the other person, rather than trying to abandon them somewhere, no matter how difficult they are."

"Hey, Kazuma, why did you look at me when you said that?"

I see—so it's understanding the other person.

"Thank you very much. I will try talking to the others tomorrow."

"No matter how useless they are, everyone has something they're good at. If you find that, they might surprise you. Even if it's someone who makes you wanna leave them in a faraway dungeon somewhere, you might see a side you didn't expect if you watch them carefully."

"Hey, like I said, why do you look my way when you say that?"

A side you didn't expect.

Speaking of, I still didn't know them that well.

"As an elite gamer to begin with, if I just think of it as a kind of handicap, something to tie me down, I don't even get mad when others hold me back. Especially with how easy life is now anyway."

Darkness petted Chomusuke with a smile as she cozied up to the cat. Hearing Kazuma's confident words, Darkness decided to answer. "Hey, Kazuma, I'm not sure you should say such lewd things around the others."

"The bondage I'm referring to isn't the private fun time that you love. Don't insult gamers."

Still, maybe this was no ordinary guy if he had been a central guild member at such a young age.

As I began to see Kazuma in a new light, Aqua spoke up while feeding Emperor Zel on her lap.

"You keep talking about us like nuisances, but surely you aren't including me in that, right? You're talking about these two, yeah?"

"...What're you flapping about? You're the biggest problem child of all."

Darkness was busy enjoying Chomusuke nibbling on her fingertip but decided to chime in.

"Hey, Kazuma, I don't cause any problems, do I? I'm confident I'm the most sensible out of the three of us..."

...Hey, wait a minute.

"Where do you get that confidence from?" Kazuma replied. "To me you all just look like mildly intelligent goblins when you're in battle."

"You wanna take this outside?" said Aqua. "You've got some nerve treating me, with my beauty and intelligence, like a goblin."

"Yeah," Darkness said, "this guy's gotten pretty full of himself recently. I can't let you call young ladies something so foul just because you put that general of the Demon King into the ground."

The two of them flew into a rage, as short-tempered as any goblin.

"Both of you are obviously problem children. I am the most level-headed and calm among all of us, with my great intellect. Being cool, calm, and collected is the selling point of Arch-wizards, after all... However, that poses a bit of a problem. I'm planning a certain something with some pains-in-the-neck who are all so different from one another that I'm not sure it'll work."

"'C-cool, calm, and collected' must be a joke. You're like a defective firework that goes off on its own without even being lit," Kazuma said.

"Hey, Megumin, I'm pretty sure I'm more levelheaded than you are, in battle at least," Aqua protested.

"I don't wanna hear that from you, Megumin! You're the most impatient of all of us!"

The three of them said something to me, but none of it reached my ears. I was busy pondering something else with my arms crossed.

2

"I have a question for you. What do you want to do more than anything right now?"

"Marry you, Megumin."

As she performed a questionable dance by herself at the hideout early the next morning, Cecily replied with immediate confidence.

"...Er, I am a girl, so marrying you would be..."

Supposedly, that questionable dance had been a prayer to the goddess Aqua. Cecily had been softly muttering, "Lady Aqua, may today also be a good day," while she moved. Then the priestess went on to say, "Unlike the hardheaded Eris Church, the Axis Church considers the walls of race and sex to be trivial, as long as there are no devil girls or undead involved, so there's no problem."

There was quite a big one.

"Um, I appreciate the sentiment, but I would like to become a bride myself. I am sorry."

"Oh well. Then I'll do what I can to be a good husband."

"No, I want to be a bride for a man! D-do not act so depressed; it is not fair for you to act sad when you are always joking around!"

Just as I was wondering what to do with Cecily as she looked at me like an abandoned puppy, she grinned.

"I swear, you're so cute, Megumin! Oh well, I heard from someone there's a legendary treasure that makes even a sex change possible. I'll do whatever it takes to get it for you."

"Even if you turn into a guy, it does not mean I will marry you, so please stop! Anyway, is there nothing else you want? You're always so full of desire, I would think there'd be a ton of things you would desire to do," I said, managing to push her away as she embraced me and stroked my cheek.

"What are you talking about? I'm an Axis follower, you know?"

"...? Of course I know! And?" I cocked my head.

"As an Axis follower, if I have something I want to do, of course I just do it without hesitating. So that I may be unashamed before Lady Aqua, I live and do as I want every day. Like this." She gave a little smirk as she clung to me.

"What you do and say is ridiculous, but I admit I thought that way of life sounded kind of cool just now. You seemed every bit the true, freedom-loving Axis follower."

"Thanks! I think your volatile way of life is pretty cool, too!"

I wish you wouldn't call it "volatile."

Then, as Cecily stroked my head…

"I'll listen if you have any worries, you know? I'm the adviser, remember?"

Per usual, she made an unexpected show of insight. Right, the problem I'd been worried about recently was…

"I didn't get a clear answer before, but you have someone you like, right, Megumin?"

Wondering how I was going to make a raid succeed with this group of second-stringers, I said, "N-n-no, what are you saying?! I'm worried about how to do a raid with these members, not something like that!"

My ears turned red at Cecily's truly unnecessary insight.

Smiling at me with such a tender expression, she somehow looked like a legit clergywoman.

This person showed an unexpected side of herself sometimes—quite unfairly, I think.

"You'll hate me if I tease you any more, so I guess I'll pretend to believe you! Right, first is the question of which noble to go after. Next is how to break in. Last is whether they're really doing bad things and if it'll cause a big incident if we do something dumb. In other words, the target should be a family that's not obscure, has money, and is likely to be doing wicked deeds in secret."

I see—I don't care for being teased, but that was an unusually useful opinion.

"Though, actually, I've had my eye on a place since I first heard your plan."

"What's going on, Cecily? You're so dependable today."

Seriously, what had happened to this person? Like that true-blue pervert Zesta, sometimes Axis followers displayed some amazing abilities. Feeling hopeful, I waited to hear who she'd had her eye on…

"Did you know the Dustiness family has a home in this town?"

"……"

As I was at a loss for words, for some reason, Cecily got even more excited.

"The bigger the target is, the better. In that respect, the Dustiness family is more than qualified. Next is whether they have money, and that family is made up of big-shot nobles who contend for first or second place in this country. There's no way they're poor."

They weren't exactly broke, but as far as nobles went, they weren't superrich, either.

"Best of all, their whole clan is supposedly made up of zealous Eris followers! As a family steeped in such wickedness, they must be up to something shady!"

"Sorry, let us not go with them. Rather, please spare me the trouble."

I was humiliated to have listened to this priestess so earnestly.

"If you say so, I guess that's that... Well then, I have a second candidate I was thinking of. Why don't we look into that for now?"

3

"The Belheim family? ...Nah, I think they'd be too hard for beginners. I haven't heard any bad rumors about them yet, and they also have tight security. I wouldn't recommend hitting them."

I swung by the Adventurers Guild sometime in the afternoon and grabbed Chris, who was hanging around, bored. I asked her about the noble family Cecily had mentioned.

"If you cannot recommend it to beginners, that kind of sounds like you are used to breaking into the homes of nobles."

"*Pfft! Cough, cough...!* Look, I'm a Thief-class adventurer, so even supposing I don't actually break in anywhere, I can at least imagine what it's like!" Chris said in a panic as she gloriously spewed the Crimson Beer that had been in her mouth.

I see. Maybe that's like Explosion spell-casters and their habit of searching out big, hard, fun-to-destroy things.

The Thief wiped her mouth with a handkerchief. "I'll go ahead and do some good research into the Belheim family, but a more small-time noble's mansion would be better at first, you know? Families at the level where they'd be done for if their misdeeds got out often don't make it public when they're robbed."

"Just asking, but that is only a guess, right? You have not ever actually broken in anywhere, have you...?"

"N-n-no? Come on, Megumin! I'd never cross such a dangerous line!"

So she said, but her eyes were shifting about like someone bad at lying.

She was restless, folding and then unfolding her handkerchief on the table suspiciously.

"...You're an Eris follower, right, Chris? Can you swear to Lady Eris that you've never done anything so dangerous as breaking into a noble's mansion alone?"

"Ummm... S-sure, I can swear that all day. I can, but... Not knowing how to respond like this is the strangest sensation...," she said, swearing plainly.

While I thought it odd of her, I was relieved. Chris seemed to be a devout Eris follower, so she couldn't have been faking it. I'd worried she'd been reckless, but it seemed my fear was unfounded.

"By the way, I have a question for you, Chris. What is the thing you want to do most—the wish you want more than anything?"

"Me?! A wish I want to come true... Hey, Megumin, you don't actually know the truth about me, right? I'm more of a wish granter than a wish grantee, but..."

Once again, she'd said something strange. I'd thought this girl was the most levelheaded in my crew of bandits. Surprisingly, that seemed to maybe not be the case.

"Actually, Kazuma told me if I want to be a good manager, I need to make sure I understand the others. I guess you could say I want to know more about you."

At that, the Thief gave me a long and curious stare.

"Huh, that's an awfully grown-up thing for Kazuma to say. Anyway, a wish I want to come true or something I want to do? Hmm, I'm already doing what I want, so I guess there's nothing at the moment."

"You are doing what you want? That is exactly what Cecily said. Perhaps Axis and Eris followers aren't that different?"

"Wait, give me another chance! I'll give it a good think before I answer!" Chris furrowed her brow and started groaning, apparently unhappy to be seen as the same as someone from the Axis Church.

After considering for a moment, Chris bashfully said, "...I want to go shopping with female friends and buy lots of clothes. Trying some delicious parfaits at a trendy shop would be nice, too... I guess mundane stuff like that is what I'd like."

Despite her tough appearance, she said something pretty girlie.

"Unlike that forever-alone Yunyun or Illis with her social standing, you could actually accomplish that. All I can imagine a well-informed bandit girl who lives as an adventurer doing is living it up, having tons of experiences."

"O-ouch! I've never even been on a date!"

When I'd first met Chris, I'd thought she was a bold Thief to challenge Kazuma so suddenly, but maybe she had a surprisingly pure side.

I see. Kazuma was exactly right.

I'd been able to see sides of both Cecily and Chris that I hadn't before. Hmm, a date?

I felt like I hadn't experienced a proper one-on-one date, either.

......

"Speaking of, it just occurred to me, but I have something else I want to ask."

"What's that? I've known Darkness a long time, and, well, plenty has happened with Aqua and me. Kazuma and I have a secret-sharing relationship, too, but you're the one person in your party I've not had many dealings with. Sure, ask away," she said cheerfully, swirling her mug around.

"What is your relationship with Kazuma?"

"...Friend, I guess."

I leaned in toward Chris, who refused to meet my gaze.

"For friends, I feel like you've been quite chummy with him recently. You said you haven't had many dealings with me, but I don't think you've had many with Kazuma, either."

"W-well, we've had plenty, like, you know, teaching my Thief skills to him! But he's really just a friend! Seriously, I don't have any special feelings for that guy, okay?"

Her desperate explanation was suspicious, and I was really curious about their secret-sharing relationship.

"I pretty much used to be Kazuma's only female acquaintance, but it strikes me that he recently started getting strangely popular. It would be well enough if you had been together a long time, but I will not let some unknown yokel snatch him away."

Chris, who'd been listening quietly, blushed just a bit and looked at me teasingly, as if in payback for everything up till now.

"Huh. Speaking of, Megumin, I heard you're getting along pretty well with Kazuma recently. Tell me, tell me, do you like him? I wanna hear how serious you are."

"I like Kazuma. As far as how serious I am...deadly."

Hearing that, Chris blushed even more and flinched.

"At first, I just thought he was a quirky oddball, but that changed over time. I realized he is a good, caring person. Then my feelings changed again, and he became someone I could feel at ease with. I guess you could say by the time I realized it, I liked him. At this point, I think of him about as much as I think of Explosion in any given day."

"I—I—I—I see! You're oddly manly, Megumin. I thought you'd be like, I guess, more unsure or embarrassed. You came at me so directly, I'm not sure how to react..."

Suddenly, it seemed like there was respect in Chris's eyes.

"And so I would like to squash any potential threats before it is too late. You really are just friends with Kazuma, right?"

"Just friends, honest! Don't make your eyes glow so red! Um, well then, I'll go look into the Belheims!"

At that, Chris flew out of the Guild in a panic, terrified of some unknown threat. I left the Adventurers Guild behind as well and set off for my next destination.

Surely, Yunyun must have brought that girl over by now.

4

"Th-this is so cute! Look, that one over there, too!"

"Yes, I've never been in a store like this; everything looks so interesting... By the way, Yunyun, don't we need to go to the hideout?"

At a main street accessory shop that was popular with girls, two people I knew well were loafing around inside.

"Don't worry. By now everyone's lazing about eating snacks. Megumin's getting mad at Cecily's sexual harassment while Chris says *Oh well* with a wry smile... That kind of sounds fun in its own way..."

"Well, why don't we get going, too? Shopping is fun, but I bet the boss would scold us if she knew what we were doing."

At Iris's comment, Yunyun twitched ever so slightly.

"T-true. Not that Megumin's scary or anything, but staying too long and making them wait would be, you know. Well, then..."

"Hey, that is quite the thing to say while you drag a younger girl around and seize the chance to fulfill your secret wishes."

Yunyun shuddered, startled at my words from behind.

She nervously turned around to face me...

"...I swear. No matter how lacking you are in friends, what are you thinking making Illis go along with you? She does not know any better, Yunyun. When I set the meeting time and trusted you to follow it, I did so because it saved on using Explosion, and this is what I get on the first day?"

"...Sorry."

En route to the hideout.

Yunyun, red to the tips of her ears, followed along with her face buried in her hands.

"I'm sure you've always wanted to go shopping with a girl your age, but why did I even send you to go meet Illis in the first place? If you want to go to the store that badly, I'll go with you next time, so please try not to do such dumb things."

Hearing that, Yunyun's expression changed to one of both surprise and hope. "R-really? You'll really go with me? My list of stores I want to visit when I get a friend someday is almost enough for three notebooks already…"

"That is too many! At least narrow it down to only a few! Anyway, I have something I want to ask you two." I tossed them the same question I had asked the other members of my crew.

"What I want to do? Um, why are you asking that all of a sudden, Megumin? I can tell you, but there probably isn't enough time in a day to list all the things I wanna do…"

"Like I said, too many! Surely you have something you really hope for, a wish you want to come true more than anything!"

At that, Yunyun's eyes flickered up to me, away, then back again. "In that case, I guess I finally want a showdown with you, Megumin," she said in a low, timid voice.

"We've already had our fateful duel. In level, reputation, and as women."

"Wait a minute, you. Setting aside level and how many of the Demon King's generals we've defeated, I'm not convinced about the 'as women' part!"

Eyes glowing red, Yunyun crossed her arms and stuck out her chest, as if to show it off.

…*Why, you little*—

"I am not talking about bodily development. When you cannot even snag a guy with such a hot body for your age, trying to vie with me is rather cheeky."

"Don't think you've won just because you're getting along okay with Kazuma! I could if I wanted to…! I-if I wanted to…"

As Yunyun's voice got lower and lower, I stuck out my own chest triumphantly.

"Look, you don't have a single male friend, right? Ahhh, was that blond punk the other day your friend? He is perfect for you, is he not? I hope you are happy together!"

"I won't let that slide even as a joke; that's the one man I could never be with! Fine, I'll show when you've crossed the line! I'm going to settle this here and now!"

Yunyun, eyes emitting red light, drew her wand from her waist.

"Wh-what, you want to do this? Fine, bring it on! Actually, I was secretly annoyed back when you pressured Kazuma to have babies with you! I'll show you here and now that you can't go seducing someone's man!"

"S-stop it! That was an accident that came of assumptions and misunderstandings, so forget about it already!"

I internally recorded another victory as Yunyun lowered her wand and yelled in embarrassment.

"How many people have made advances on Kazuma?!" Iris asked. "He stripped off Chris's underwear in public, and I hear he did something indecent to Lalatina. Now b-baby-making with Yunyun...?!"

"Stop iiit! That's not true; I don't have any such feelings for Kazuma! A-a-anyway, I wanna hear about your wish, Illis! Look, Megumin does, too, right?!"

Iris blushed as Yunyun desperately tried to change the topic.

"I—I, well..."

...These people.

"I—I want to...with Kazuma...!"

"I will not let you say any more! What is it with you people? Are all of you lovesick? Is that normal for girls of this generation?!"

5

A most unusual spectacle greeted my eyes when I returned to the hideout with the two girls suffering from heartache.

"For an Eris follower, you have quite an eye. That's right; Lady Aqua is sublime. And she is very lovely."

"Yeah, well, I don't think she's a bad person. Sure."

Cecily was giving some kind of sermon to Chris, who sat holding her knees on the carpet.

Evidently, the priestess was explaining about Aqua's virtues.

"Welcome back, Megumin. I was just trying to convert Chris to be an Axis follower."

"Huh?! Wait a minute! I'm pretty sure I'm not gonna convert!"

Although she'd been listening to the speech, Chris seemed surprised to hear something so unexpected.

"What are you talking about? Then let me ask: What do you think about devils and the undead?"

"Obviously, I think they should go to Hell."

Cecily smiled broadly at Chris's confident, immediate answer.

"That's wonderful! Chris, you do have what it takes to be an Axis follower after all! Yes, just as Lady Aqua decreed: We shall kill devils, strike down the Demon King, and return the undead to the dirt! So? How about it? Why don't you join the Axis Church, too…?!"

"The Eris Church does also teach that devils and the undead are to be abhorred, you know?! I never thought the day would come when I would be invited to join the Axis Church. Why do I keep falling into such weird situations recently?!"

I had thought that, being Axis and Eris followers, they'd get into a fight, but luckily, the two of them seemed to be on surprisingly good terms.

Beckoning for the two followers of opposing faiths to come over, I proceeded to discuss my plans with everyone.

I was standing in front of a table, so I thrust both hands onto it and clambered on top.

"Well then, everyone, thank you for coming. Our thief gang has acquired a hideout, earned supporters, and procured a regular source of income. As for personnel, we are currently swamped with applicants. This is certainly a most delightful situation."

"Yeah. We're getting together more often, too, so we're very much on track," Yunyun said, nodding at my words.

"Yes, right now things are going smoothly. With everything taking shape, I have decided we should finally get to work for real."

At that, Iris cocked her head.

"'Work'? What exactly are we doing today? The other day, we went to the mountain to pick leaves, and before that we went to the river to fish, but I didn't have any box lunches made today. If we're to go out, how about tomorrow?"

"Who said we are going to hang out?! Now, admittedly, it was feeling like I don't know what kind of group this is anymore, but please do not lose sight of our original goal. Think back. Why did we get together in the first place?"

At my words, each of them opened their mouths one after another.

"I thought it was to make friends…"

"I thought it was to go on adventures…"

"I was enticed because I wanted cute, pretty little girls to surround and fawn over me."

"Huh?! This is a bit different from what I heard!"

I pounded the table with a *wham-wham*. They'd all completely forgotten our real reason for forming this crew.

"No! I tended to get off track here and there, too, but our original goal was to support the Silver-Haired Thief Brigade's actions and to try to assist them! Raids! We must raid crooked nobles and make them know our name! And so, Chris, please tell us the results of your investigation!"

"They're clean. They don't seem to be doing anything particularly bad, so I don't think we should make them the target. Or, rather, why did you decide on them in the first place?"

At Chris's report, Cecily said glumly, "When I went to them begging for donations to the Axis Church, they told me, 'We have our own religion.' They said, 'We don't want anything to do with shady groups like the Eris or Axis Church.'"

At that, Chris suddenly flew into a rage.

"We need to hit them! Heathens calling us shady need to be taught a lesson!"

"Let's do it; let's do it! You get it, Chris. I knew you were a true Axis devotee underneath that Eris guise! How about it, Megumin?"

Though they got excited, I said, "It's not okay at all. We must not raid them if they are not doing anything wrong—let us choose another family. Lady Aqua and Lady Eris would not forgive it."

"She would forgive it; Lady Eris would sooo forgive it!"

"I'm sure Lady Aqua would overlook it, too! In fact, you'd most definitely hear a divine voice that bids you, *Raid away!*"

What am I going to do with these two weirdos?

Chris really shocked me. I had thought she was more levelheaded than that.

I really felt the importance of actually getting to know your companions, as Kazuma had said.

"Oh, I think I understand now. So we're going to stand up for justice at last! Then let's do this: There's actually something called a 'list of nobles' whom the royal family has their eyes on. Let's go ahead and raid the mansion of a noble on that list, and if nothing turns up, then we'll have my father apologize…"

"You must stay a good girl! You cannot bring your father into this!"

As I was calling out Iris for offering an even more extreme suggestion, Yunyun gave a few tugs on my cape.

"Can't we just be happy we have a group that meets up for fun every day? Look, like these snacks Illis's maid made for us. They're delicious; you try some, too, Megumin… Wai— Aaaahhh!"

I tossed all the snacks Yunyun offered me into my mouth, and when I finished devouring them…

"Oh well, no matter how much we want to raid, we cannot do anything without a target. Let us watch and wait for a while."

After all, I'd resolved not to cause a ruckus by myself as I usually did. This time, I had to be responsible because I was the boss.

"Who said you could eat my portion, tooooo?!"

I was deep in contemplation as Yunyun shook me back and forth.

6

"…I'm home!"

"Welcome home. You look a bit tired."

In the end, time flew by and we never came to an actual decision.

Chris had offered to find another noble who it'd be okay to steal from, so we'd packed it in for the day, but…

"Ah, I was just thinking how hard it is to understand and manage people. Between one woman teasing me, someone I thought was levelheaded being surprisingly over-the-top, getting into fights with a self-proclaimed rival, and realizing that a little girl is still after you, I am pretty worn out."

Usually, I was the one unleashing mayhem, so I hadn't thought it would be this tiring being the one trying to stop it.

"I'm not sure what all that's about, but it seems tough. Hopefully it helps you realize what I have to go through."

Tossing myself onto the sofa next to where Kazuma was relaxing, I gazed up at him.

"Oh, what's this? Staring at me like the girl adventurers in the Guild do these days? Have you finally noticed how charming I am?" He spoke with sarcastically furrowed brow and flared nostrils, like he was trying to look cool.

Maybe I wasn't one to talk, but why was Iris attracted to this guy?

"You sure have been popular with the girls at the Adventurers Guild recently. They were calling you Easy-ma, since they only had to butter you up a little to get you to buy them drinks."

"Remember their faces. I'll use Steal on them next time we meet."

Gnashing his teeth, Kazuma had no problem making creepy remarks about other women, even with me right next to him.

Why was I into this guy?

I recalled the exchange I'd had with my grunts earlier that day.

Though I'd said Iris and Yunyun were lovesick, if I could somehow forgive this fickle boy, could it be that I was the one who was blinded by love?

Kazuma was habitually lazy, bad-mouthed others despite being a wimp, and bragged about his accomplishments at the Adventurers Guild without a shred of humility.

He had average looks, and personality-wise, he was a coward who was neither fantastically good nor bad.

"...Hey, really now, what's going on? I can't help getting a bit embarrassed when you're staring at me so hard. What? Do you like me?"

Also, despite being a total perv, he got flustered when I looked at him like this.

And just by showing a little interest...

"I do. I myself was seriously wondering why I like you so much."

"Huh?!"

You see, this was how he acted.

"H-how many times have I told you not to say such things so flippantly and out of the blue like that? I gotta be prepared first. From now on, give me advance notice with a letter or something. I need a month, a day, and what time you're planning on saying something like that."

"What kind of mood-killing confession would that be? I just always say what I want to. It is like you told me yesterday, right? That I should try to understand others? I was trying to understand you just now, Kazuma."

He fidgeted as I said that while looking straight into his eyes.

I couldn't help smiling as I watched him. "You're able to give me good directions because you understand me, right? Do you know what I'm thinking right now? Do you know what I want to do with you, alone, together like this?"

"...Se—"

Hey.

"No, wait, what I said just now doesn't count!"

"Uh-uh, let us hear what you were going to say while the mood was so nice, in front of a young girl!"

Seeing Kazuma, who held his tongue in a fluster when he saw the color of my eyes, I felt sort of weird for having gotten so caught up in my head.

Raiding with a perfectly prepared plan wasn't like me.

Managing everyone and stopping them, thinking about what was to come... None of this was like me at all.

I always just gave it my all.

What on earth had I been worrying about?

"No, Megumin, I don't think that sort of questioning is fair. Like, if you gave me three choices, I'd definitely know the answer. Give me another chance."

I'd feel guilty always relying on him, but if things got too hairy for me to handle on my own, this guy would help me if I asked him to.

Kazuma was still babbling about something stupid. I just said, "No, it's fine."

I smiled to show I wasn't mad anymore.

...However...

"Wait. I said I'm sorry; forgive me! I'll think about it again, seriously this time! ...Of course! That would've been taking things too quickly. First, maybe a kiss..."

"I told you it's fine! Anyway, lower your voice! Aqua and Darkness are in the kitchen; if they see us like this...!"

No sooner had I said that than...

...I realized Kazuma wasn't looking at me.

"Oh nonono..."

What Kazuma was looking at was a figure poking her head out from the hallway, grasping a rag with both hands as if she'd come to wipe the table—Aqua.

She backed up as she stared with a look of horror...

"Hey, Darkness, this is bad! Kazuma and Megumin are sitting close to each other, red-faced and talking about kissing or something!"

I stopped Aqua in a panic as she tried to go snitch.

7

The next day.

We'd all gathered together in the hideout. I whirled my mantle in front of my minions.

"I am fired up today! And with this good weather, it is a fine day for a B and E!"

Striking a cool pose, I took my favorite staff in hand.

"Hey, just asking, but we're sneaking into a mansion to steal from a crooked noble, right? What's a B and E? I'm not sure what that means, but it somehow sounds dangerous...," Yunyun said, looking worried.

"It is exactly what it sounds like. I learned it from Kazuma; he said it was a term you use during a raid or whatever. Why don't we go to the noble's mansion for now, and we can wing it the rest of the way?"

"Hey, we're a thief gang, right? We're a group of thieves, not robbers, right?!"

I thought it best to ignore Yunyun, who had grabbed me by the shoulders. Instead, I turned to Chris. "Well, did you find a target worth hitting, like you were saying yesterday?"

"Y-yeah, more or less. Not to sound like Yunyun, but we're going in to steal, right? We aren't mugging them, right?"

Shaking a bit, Chris took out a map outlining the town of Axel. The girl pointed a finger at a forest outside of town.

"Um, actually, a certain rich person has their second home nearby. Something strange is definitely going on around there."

According to Chris, there had been eyewitness accounts of monsters near that house that were stronger than anything found near Axel.

"Is that not the jurisdiction of the Adventurers Guild? I heard recently that Axel's adventurers are not working at all because they made a small fortune from hunting the stronger monsters over and over for their rewards. Maybe that caused a migration of stronger monsters that prey on weaker ones?"

At that, Chris shook her head with a conflicted look.

"That might be true, but it might not. There could be a Sacred Treasure that's being used at that house."

That Sacred Treasure was a supposedly powerful item that could summon random monsters and bind them into service.

If that was true, such a name would certainly be an apt one, but...

"Could a noble I have never even heard of really get their hands on such an amazing thing? I would not be surprised if it went for a ridiculous price."

"Well, you see, actually, that artifact was sealed away—sunk to the bottom of a lake where a wicked and powerful bounty monster slept—so that no one could ever find it."

A wicked and powerful bounty monster.

...Suddenly, I recalled something like that had been vanquished in a lake near Axel recently.

"Yes, the Kowloon Hydra. It absorbed the magical power of the land, polluting even the trees. Apparently, they sealed the artifact there, thinking no one would ever come close to a place like that, but... The vegetation around the lake returned much sooner than expected, and people started to visit. Then the person who had sealed the artifact away tried dredging it up from the bottom of the lake to move it somewhere safer, but..."

"I see. Someone else had already stolen it."

The eyewitness info about powerful monsters appearing only added to the validity of the story. Actually, when I thought about it, it was odd someone would build a mansion there, rather than inside a walled town.

Supposedly, they were summoning monsters at random, too, so when any appeared that they didn't like, maybe they were chucking them into the forest.

"Also, about that artifact… For some reason, it seems to find its way into the hands of nasty, wealthy people a lot—its former owner was a middle-aged lord named Alderp."

Ah, that man who was always obsessed with Darkness and went missing.

"As royalty, I cannot allow such a dangerous item to be out there. Let's go there for sure, boss!"

"Hey, Illis, did you just say you were royalty?"

"No, I didn't." Iris backed away slowly from Yunyun's serious expression.

Then Cecily, who had been sitting quietly on the sofa sipping tea, said, "I could use something like that…that Sacred Treasure thing. I would summon a monster and, after making it rampage about, Axis followers would join by the hundreds. Yes, I bet recruitment numbers would double just like that!"

Huh, I guess there are ways to abuse it.

It seemed more and more like an item we had to do something about. Although, wasn't this going to be a pretty risky venture? It seemed too momentous, like something we couldn't handle ourselves—it already felt like a bad sign.

Still…

"I am certain recovering dangerous divine artifacts was one of the Silver-Haired Thief Brigade's goals. Let us try hitting that house!"

…It was a smallish mansion, visibly spotless, as if it had only just been built.

As apparent anti-monster defenses, the outside of the mansion was surrounded by a sturdy iron fence. Within, numerous traps had been laid, as well.

Sure, that was good and all, but…

"Well, this place sure is a sight."

"Hey, this is not the time for that kind of talk! We have to help right away!"

The noble mansion that we had been planning to raid was at that very moment getting attacked by a bunch of monsters.

"Oh no, maybe they summoned some monsters they couldn't control! Even then, it would be strange for the monster swarm to be attacking."

As Chris calmly observed the situation next to me, Iris drew her sword.

"Either way, shouldn't we go rescue them? This has to be too much for their guards alone…" The princess turned to me for direction.

I looked over the scene; guards were fighting back from behind the fence, using spears and bows.

However…

"No, I have an idea. We should let them be!" Cecily suddenly blurted out.

"True. As a thief gang, checking things out a bit is the right answer. After all, if they really have the Sacred Treasure, they'll probably bring it out to try to control the monsters."

Even Chris was on board.

"Great minds think alike, even if you are an Eris follower! Yes, we shouldn't interfere until the last moment, and once they're in real trouble, we'll help them as patronizingly as possible! At that point, there'll be fewer monsters, making it easier to rescue them, too!"

"No, that's not why I said it! I just meant that to do this like true bandits, we should check if the thing we're after is even here or not…!"

Sure, sure. Cecily nodded at a flustered Chris. "Then in return for our help, we demand that powerful item we searched for, right? Always crafty, you Eris followers! I can't say I mind that sort of thing, though!"

"N-n-n-no—! I never said we should wait that late to help…!"

I could understand what Chris was saying. Indeed, if they really had this Sacred Treasure thing, they'd use it if they got into trouble.

We could save ourselves the risky business of sneaking deep into the mansion to find its location if we just waited it out.

"I did not think you were such a cruel person, Chris, but, well, it is not a bad idea."

"You too, Megumin?! No, listen here, both of you!"

It was at that moment when…

"I told you—let's not live in a place like this!"

"It's too late for that; that young lady always gets her way!"

Hearing the voices of guards from the other side of the fence, Yunyun and Iris gave me a worried look.

"Where is she?! We have to at least make sure she gets out safe…"

"I haven't seen her! We've got to stay to make sure."

Having heard the plight, I turned to my crew. "If we go up against that many monsters, even we might not get out unscathed."

"Megumin…," Yunyun muttered softly at my hushed statement.

Not responding to her, I kept my eyes on the creatures assailing the manor and continued quietly. "Also, I am the boss of this thief gang, so I have a responsibility to try to keep everyone out of danger. You are an intelligent Crimson Magic Clan member yourself, so I'm sure you can see that leaving them alone to see what happens is the wise option."

Seeming to understand that, Yunyun shut up, looking dejected. Iris, sword drawn as she stood at my side, looked back and forth between me and the mansion. Turning my back on the two of them, I took a step forward.

"For me, however, being an adventurer comes before being the boss of a bandit crew. Since I intend to eventually defeat the Demon King, I cannot simply watch and wait while there are monsters in front of me," I declared, taking up a stance with my staff. Someone let out a quiet laugh from behind me.

"Huh. Being an adventurer is more up your alley than being in a thief gang."

Chris's words didn't sound like praise, yet she seemed somehow pleased. Listening to her giggles, I began to chant. I'd wanted to be like those people I admired so much, but oh well.

I could never stand by with monsters right in front of me.

"Megumin, let me handle any monsters you miss. I'll pick them all off!"

As I chanted, Yunyun gleefully took a stance behind me on my right side, her wand readied.

It was bold of her to assume that there would be anything left after I was done.

"When you cast the spell, some of them are sure to come this way. Let me handle the ones that do! Today, I am your shield, boss!"

I felt like this girl was the one most worthy of protecting. Oblivious to such things, Iris stood behind me on my left, sword held in her hands.

"Then I will help you from the back! I'll heal you nice and slow if you get hurt, so make sure you let me know!"

Everyone smiled unconsciously at Cecily, a woman who was unwavering, even in this situation.

Chris drew her dagger to cover me.

"Well then, I guess I'll get serious, too. I'll show you what a Thief can do. All right, Megumin, let's do this!"

Maybe we could come together as a thief gang a little later—yes, like after the Demon King was defeated and peace had returned.

"Look, I'll let you do the honors, so go all out, boss," Yunyun urged provocatively.

In response...

"Explooosion—!!"

I unleashed my spell with all my might...!

8

After my mana recovered enough for me to walk, I plodded back home to the mansion.

"Welcome home! Listen to this, Megumin! We're having speckled crab for the first time in a while! Reminds you of when we first moved here, doesn't it?!"

Aqua welcomed me back with a big smile as she made the pincers of the crab in her hands go *snip-snip*.

"Well, that is a treat. I never thought I would get to eat speckled crab again in my life."

Dragging my languid, mana-deficient body along, I collapsed onto the sofa.

"You seem even more exhausted than usual today. I heard the boom all the way from here, but it felt a bit different. I didn't see it with my eyes, but I'll give today's Explosion ninety-five points," Kazuma said excitedly from where he was seated at the table.

"Speaking of, Megumin, you look kind of pleased. Did something good happen?" Darkness asked with a kind face as she placed a boiling pot on the table.

"Well, today it became very clear what I want to do more than anything. That must be the reason."

"There's something you wanna do besides cast Explosion?"

Kazuma put a damper on my enthusiasm with an unnecessary interruption.

I wish he'd finally stop thinking of me as just an Explosion girl.

All I did today was take everyone to the noble's mansion and cast Explosion to help the people there, as monsters attacked them for some reason...

"...Wait, was casting Explosion all I did today?"

"What's up with you all of a sudden? Anyway, isn't it a little late to be asking that? All you ever do is use that spell, right? If you took away that spell, the only thing that'd be left is the loli part of you."

I looked Kazuma up and down. He was pouring booze into a glass with a *glug-glug*. This man had just called me something disgusting.

"Then you are a loli-lover for coming on to me every now and then. I'll let everyone at the Adventurers Guild know about Loli-ma."

"C-cut it out—don't take me down with you. You'll be officially known as a loli yourself."

Ignoring us, Aqua wasted no time putting the crabs on the grill.

"Sheesh, what are the two of you thinking, arguing with amazing food in front of you? Can't you live like me, calm and relaxed?"

"Didn't you just cry when you stubbed your toe on the sofa, after you jumped around all thrilled about getting seafood from Darkness's dad?"

I was about to wash up for dinner when Darkness came to lend a hand after she put the pot on the table.

"I don't know what happened, but you seem especially perky. Why don't you tell me what you did today while we eat? Seems like you've been having a lot of fun recently, Megumin," the blond woman said with a laugh.

...In the end, the noble we'd helped had been, in a word, awful.

After we'd eradicated the monsters, a young lady of the house had appeared. She was about our age and had apparently fled from the mansion by herself.

She'd promptly told us she hadn't even asked for our help, despite us not asking for thanks.

If I hadn't been completely dry on mana and unable to move, I probably would've found myself assaulting her.

Why was that place being attacked to begin with?

Chris had said we'd have the answers sooner or later, even if we were left with questions now, as the Silver-Haired Thief Brigade also had their eye on that noble's residence.

I'd been curious as to how Chris could've possibly known that. Probably through some sort of bandit information network.

"Well said, Darkness. Actually, I've been wondering what Megumin's been getting into, as well—probably up to some nonsense again." Kazuma spoke without taking his eyes off the sizzling crabs.

"I know," Aqua said. "I heard from Cecily. She said she'd thought up some way of earning easy money by using pretty little girls."

Kazuma and Darkness gave me a look that said they couldn't believe I'd been roped into something that sketchy.

"Do not worry—I will tell you all what I was doing. It wasn't anything unsavory... I mean it, okay?! You don't have to look at me like that!"

After I gave a flustered explanation for myself, I recalled the day's events. The result had been lame and a bit frustrating, but I couldn't help but feel it was all good as long as the heroic thieves I admired so deeply took care of things for us.

If things went as I hoped...

"Everything started on the night of the fireworks show. I escaped the clutches of the police, and as I was heading back to the mansion alone..."

If only I could meet those people I look up to, even just one more time...

Final
Chapter

The
Thief
Gang
Strikes
Back

1

It happened the day we set out for the neighboring country of Elroad. That was some time after returning to Axel after a bunch of stuff had happened.

"So this is the Donnelly residence. I don't know why they built it in the middle of nowhere, but it seems like a pretty nice place."

We'd come to the home of a noble family. The structure was built right in the middle of a forest near the town of Axel.

I looked up at the manor, muttering. Darkness, who was all dressed up to meet the nobles, nodded gently.

"The Donnellys have been involved in commerce for years. They may not be as prestigious, but they beat my family financially. I don't like the girl who heads the family, though. Every time we meet at social events, her words are dripping with disdain for my house, calling us penniless plebs, even though she's an upstart! Kazuma, there might be something more to this quest than meets the eye. Be careful, all right?"

Darkness was, apparently, not overly fond of these nobles. Aqua, who'd also been forced to wear a dress, likewise raised her voice in anger.

"I know about the Donnellys! When my pocket money ran out and

I went to borrow from a lender they operate, they kicked me out, saying they don't lend to Axis followers!"

"You did that when I was gone? ...Geez. As if Darkness trying to take my virginity by drugging me in Elroad wasn't enough... You both need to learn from Megumin's recent good behavior."

"?!"

Megumin jumped in surprise at my words.

"...Hey. Did you get up to something recently?"

"No."

As Megumin's flat, eye-averting denial convinced me she definitely had done something, Darkness said, "K-Kazuma... I'll apologize for drugging you, so can you just forget about it and pretend like it never happened already...? I mean, we're both embarrassed and ashamed, right? Yeah? I'll, uh, buy you some nice wine when we get home, so..."

"Hey, Kazuma, this family won't do; let's turn them down! Nothing good can come from a family that's prejudiced against Axis followers!"

Ignoring the nosier members of the group, I knocked on the mansion door...

...A letter had arrived for me.

It was a quest, addressed to the most famous adventurer in Axel.

I understood why someone would want to depend on me after I'd made a legend of myself again over in Elroad.

I was something of a busy man, however, training body and soul for the confrontation with the Demon King.

Previously I had refused such requests, but this time it had come from a nobleman.

I already had lots of connections, but as I had only just recently learned how wonderful power was, I decided that having new ones couldn't be all that bad.

With that in mind, I had accepted the quest, but...

"Nice to meet you. I am Karen, the head of the Donnelly family."

It was a young redheaded girl, just a little older than I was, who came to greet us in the drawing room.

Close to my height, she was a beauty, possessing the slender figure of a model.

"You are Mr. Kazuma Satou, yes? Thank you very much for coming today to hear about my family's requ—"

The person calling herself Karen froze as she looked my way.

No, it was as she looked at Megumin, who was hiding behind me.

"...Excuse me, please wait one moment."

"C-certainly... I don't mind, but..."

I grabbed Megumin, who was still huddled at my back, by the scruff of her neck and went out to the hall for a moment.

"What happened between you and that Karen chick? Out with it."

"What are you talking about? Nothing happened; I have never even met her before... All right, I will tell you, so don't Drain Touch me! I won't be able to cast today's Explosion if you do!"

Megumin had been acting suspiciously ever since we arrived at the mansion. She spoke while keeping an eye on my right hand as it came closer to her.

"...Actually, my companions and I helped this family out when they were getting attacked by monsters before..."

I had no clue why Megumin had been in the middle of a forest like this, but it didn't really seem like she was hiding anything as she spoke.

"Seriously, I thought you were gonna add on a bit about how you destroyed part of the mansion when you killed the monsters with Explosion, or that you obliterated their guards along with the monsters."

"No, nothing quite like that, but..." Megumin was still being a little evasive for some reason.

"Shouldn't you be more confident if you have nothing on your conscience? What, are you worried because you were killing monsters behind our backs? It does concern me, but from what I hear, your companions or whoever aren't weak, right?"

"Yes, a fairly strong grunt and a friendless Crimson Magic Clan member. There's also an Axis Church priestess and a Thief."

It was a bit of an odd party composition, but the friendless Crimson

Magic Clan member must've been Yunyun, and if she was with Megumin, there wasn't much cause for concern.

"No problem, then. Getting EXP is important, after all—I'll even go with you when I have free time."

"All you ever have is free time. Well, since you've offered, I guess I will let you in, too. I am sure you will be surprised."

Megumin wasn't really making sense, but at least it sounded like she was having fun.

With Explosion Girl in tow, I opened the door to the drawing room once more, and...

"Apologize! Apologize to me for kicking me out because you refuse to lend money to Axis followers!"

"M-my apologies. I, er, do apologize for that worker..."

Aqua was forcing an apology out of Karen, while Darkness hid her bright-red face with both hands. Honestly, I just wanted to leave right then and there.

2

"...You want us to eradicate monsters wandering in the mansion's vicinity?"

"Yes. With your skill as famed adventurers of this town, we feel assured in requesting this of your party, Mr. Satou..."

After quieting the sulking Aqua with tea cakes, we were given the rundown.

"Well, that's true. It's quite a high reward, though, isn't it? Can I take that to mean you think highly of us?"

"Mind trying to be a little humbler? Besides, I told you in the beginning, didn't I? Be careful, since there might be more to this family's request than meets the eye...," Darkness whispered, elbowing my stomach as I listened to Karen with a straight face.

Considering our accomplishments, our reputation up until now was undeserved—this was the right way to treat us.

As for Karen, at my small display of confidence, she suddenly grasped my hand with both of hers.

"Of course, Mr. Satou—I have heard such good things about you. With your various skills and wonderfully quick wit, they say you have made a fool of many of the Demon King's generals. I have also heard that your companions are all advanced classes like Arch-priest and Arch-wizard…!"

"Well, that's true. If I hadn't been here, who knows what would have happened to this town…?"

Embarrassed though I was as Karen held my hand and looked up at me while she spoke, I did my best to seem even more self-assured.

Appearing disgusted, Darkness said, "…Hey, I belong to Kazuma's party, too." The blond woman spoke bluntly and with a distant, angry stare.

"Oh dear, I thought you had just come along in a cheeky attempt to keep me from taking this cordial gentleman away… I suppose the rumors that you were playing adventurer were true, Miss Dustiness. It must be very hard to be from a family with no money, and whose only saving grace is their social standing." Karen laughed while she slipped her fingers out from mine.

"Huh, that's a funny thing to say. Just as I'd expect from an upstart noble, it looks like you have no manners or modesty. Unlike an obscure, irresponsible social climber who'd probably sell their body for money, my family is prominent enough to have what you'd call aristocratic obligations. I put my body on the line as a shield for the people."

Totally unlike when she was curled up and poking me with her elbow, Darkness straightened her back slowly and smiled, emanating an aura of refinement and dignity.

…*Uh, what? This is scary.*

"Oh, goodness me, just as I would expect from you, Miss Dustiness. It moves me to think you would live in such poverty as to reuse the same dress over and over at social events for the sake of these so-called obligations. If you do not mind my hand-me-downs, why not take a few of my dresses?" Karen said. There was no smile in her eyes.

"Just as I would expect from a family who throws away dresses after one use, you're generous both in belly and spirit. But don't worry—it wasn't that I didn't have any money; I just liked wearing my mother's old dress. Besides…" Darkness crossed her arms in front of her chest. "With one of your dresses…I don't think my boobs would fit." The blond adventurer's mouth was twitching while she replied.

She hadn't even used a metaphor! Things suddenly felt really awkward.

…*What? This is seriously scary.*

I just wanted to go home.

Pounding the table with a *wham*, Karen stood up suddenly.

"Try saying that again, Dustiness—your body is the only thing you've got! All the gentlemen prefer slender women like me!!"

"Huh, even occasionally attending social events, it seems like I get more looks from men than you. Is it just my imagination? It's hard fixing a dress every time your boobs get bigger, you know. Is that not why you buy a new dress every time, too, Miss Donnelly?"

Darkness stood up as well; she had her arms folded across her midsection to accentuate her bust.

"Ahhh, they're so, so heavy… If I didn't have an adventurer's muscles, I wouldn't be able to support them, they're so heavy."

"Y-you little!"

Gnashing her teeth, Karen glared at Darkness, who made a show of furrowing her brow and appearing troubled.

"You're looking at these so jealously, Miss Donnelly, but there's nothing good about them being big, you know? They're so heavy, they make my shoulders ache, and I can only wear certain clothes. I have to get armor specially made, and they draw the eye of many gentlemen, just like… H-hey, I thought you were gonna look, but you don't know how to hold back at all, do you…?" The blond woman backed up a bit as I stared hard at what she presented.

"Ow! H-hey, what was that for? I wasn't trying to provoke you, Megumin…! I'm sorry, so stop pulling my hair!" Seemingly a bit

satisfied at seeing Megumin starting to pull Darkness's hair from behind for some reason, Karen sighed.

"U-ummm... Well then, will you accept my quest?" she asked me, putting on a smile.

3

The next day.

Having decided to take the job, we had gotten our equipment in order and come back to the site of the mansion.

We had agreed to eradicate the powerful monsters lurking nearby, but...

"But why are these tough enemies only spawning here? I wonder if there's tasty food growing here or something. Anyway, I've got a bad feeling about this. Why don't we go home and do this another day?"

We were patrolling the mansion vicinity, on the lookout for monsters.

"Didn't you say you had a bad feeling the other day, when it was raining and I tried to get you to go shopping for dinner, and then you played games, saying you weren't going outside? Do monsters even change their habitats? We accepted the quest, but it just vaguely states the targets are powerful monsters in the vicinity of the manor. If they were undead, I'd have the perfect bait to lure them in, but..."

"Hey, just asking, but that bait's not me, is it?"

Aqua tugged a few times on my sleeve, but naturally, such a question didn't need answering.

...However.

"I didn't think you'd say something like that," I said. "Your title as a well-mannered young noblewoman finally vanished in an instant, huh? What was it you said, 'It seems like I get more looks from men than you,' or something? What's that about? I guess you don't mind getting ogled like that at social events, huh?"

"N-not like tha—! No, events like that have a sort of nobleman's diplomacy that involves such gazing...," Darkness said, panicking at my words.

"Indeed. And that was the first time I saw you acting so provocatively, Darkness, with all the chest thumping and breast swaying. I see. So we just did not know you were capable of that. How did it go again? 'Ahhh, they're so, so heavy... If I didn't have an adventurer's muscles, I wouldn't be able to support them, they're so heavy,' was it? You looked so smug, too."

At Megumin's follow-up blow, Darkness turned crimson and quickened her pace.

Drawing the sword at her waist, she sliced away at the forest underbrush, as if to take out her anger.

That was when...

"Hmm? Hey, wait a second."

A faint presence triggered my Sense Foe skill and I tugged on Darkness's mantle...

"What, Kazuma? If you wanna humiliate me any more than you already have, then I'll—"

Mid-sentence, the blade of Darkness's great sword flew into the air with a resounding metallic *clang*. If she'd gone any farther, she'd be where the sword was now, herself. Realizing as much, Darkness cast aside the broken hilt and spread out both her hands to protect us. There was no sign of anything hidden in the brush ahead, however.

At times like this...

"It's coming from above! Watch out!"

As I turned my head upward, I shoved Darkness away...!

...I was in a white room that I was all too familiar with.

In front of my eyes stood Eris, looking troubled, like she had something to say.

"...Ummm."

"...Sorry. Can you please just not say anything right now?"

I sat down where I was, hiding my face as I hugged my knees to my chest.

Recalling the moment I'd declared loudly and straight-faced that it was coming from above, I just wanted to die of embarrassment.

...Well, I really had died, but still.

"I swear it's usually from overhead..."

Yet, when I'd looked up, there had been nothing. Nothing ahead and no sign of anything to the sides. With no other options, that meant...

"You've gotta be kidding me; it came from below? I really hate this world..."

When I had shoved Darkness away, some antlion like monster had suddenly crawled out from the ground, and I...

"...Lady Eris. Are you by any chance trying not to laugh? You can just let it out."

"—No! I am not stifling anything; it's fine! Wait, saying 'it's fine' doesn't make sense, either—I would never do something so imprudent when someone has died!"

Getting attacked from the opposite direction that I'd warned everyone about loudly was utterly mortifying.

Eris expertly kept a straight face, although her shoulders were twitching.

"Well, whatever... Anyway, why do you think something that strong is near the town of Axel? I'm a decently leveled adventurer, but I got one-shot."

At that, Eris's shoulders suddenly stopped trembling.

"About that... Kazuma, are you free this evening?" she asked, gazing at me with a placid expression.

"Free? Well, I am free all the time, every day. What, you want to sneak into my chambers? We can take care of that right now if you want."

"No, I am requesting your assistance in finding a Sacred Treasure! Teasing a goddess means you're gonna get smote, you know?!"

Again with that?

"That's fine, too, I guess… Wait, could the treasure have something to do with…?"

Eris shook her head slowly at my somewhat disappointed words.

"No, we cannot be sure yet… However, there is something that worries me."

…A lord called Alderp was the one who'd originally possessed the Sacred Treasure.

An item that allowed control of randomly summoned monsters, the Sacred Treasure was supposed to have been sealed away by Chris at the bottom of a lake, but…

"I had thought no one would be able to live near the lake where the Kowloon Hydra had made its lair for some time. The area had lost its magic, after all… However, for some reason, the magic and vegetation recovered sooner than expected, and people started reclaiming the land; they even started living there. Thus, I tried to dredge up that powerful item from the lake bed. I'd hoped to move it before the townspeople found it, but…"

"It was already gone."

"Yes…"

Eris, who was normally all sweet smiles or business, looked deflated.

I see. So that brings us to the current commotion with the sudden appearance of powerful monsters.

From what I'd heard, that Karen girl had loads of money, so there was a strong possibility the object in question had fallen into her hands.

It was reasonable to think she'd set up an estate in the forest, away from town, and was summoning monsters like you'd open loot boxes. Any she didn't want, the young woman would just release into the wild.

…I felt like the timing of the treasure's disappearance and of Karen's forest mansion construction didn't match up, but this was a parallel world with magic. A magic mansion, created as easily as instant food, could have been used to make that house. Exactly like what Darkness had shown me on the way to Elroad.

Unlike another, useless goddess, it was rare for Eris to make mistakes. Even so, she was my boss, the one person I respected and admired in this world.

"Very well. Basically, you're going to investigate if the artifact is at that Karen girl's home, right? I'll help you."

Eris's face lit up when I accepted. Then she made a face a bit like a kid who'd thought up a prank for some reason.

"Tonight, I will bring along another who will help us, Kazuma. As for whom…it's a secret," she said and playfully put an index finger to her lips.

4

"'…It's coming from above! Watch out!' Pretty choice last words to say right before you got killed by something below you, Kazuma. Welcome back!"

Aqua gave me a cheery smile right after my resurrection; I wanted to smack this goddess who only ever made mistakes.

Apparently, my head had been on her lap. Getting up, I surveyed my surroundings.

"Oh, you're awake, Kazuma. Er…thanks for saving me back there. Really, I'm supposed to be the shield. Sorry."

Darkness, breathing heavily under her dent-riddled armor, knelt down next to me.

When I looked, an antlion-like monster was lying with its sharp jaws broken, crushed as if violently strangled.

To think a girl who looked like this was capable of such a thing…

"I'm glad you tried to protect me, but trust my defenses a bit more next time… Wh-what are you looking at me like that for, Kazuma? I mean, what kind of face is that?"

Darkness looked puzzled at my slightly disturbed gaze.

"No, I was just thinking maybe you should forget weapons and go barehanded already. Yeah, you're an advanced attacker-type class and at a high level, to boot. I bet you could strangle a bear to death with your bare hands by now."

Darkness was startled at my still-disturbed words.

"N-no, Kazuma! Even I can't strangle a monster as tough as that to death with mere strength alone! Aqua cast an extra-powerful support spell to avenge the gruesome way you perished!" the blond woman said in a panic, apparently not wanting to be thought of as a muscle-bound girl.

"The horrific way I died—exactly how did I go this time? It happened so fast, I don't remember."

"You were torn clean in two, from the top of your head down to your crotch…"

"I can't hear you; I can't hear you! Hey, wait a second—my death was that gory? …Ah, I was wondering why my clothes were fine despite being torn in half—somebody changed them!"

Wait, who did that?

Darkness and Megumin hastily averted their faces when I looked their way.

What kind of reaction is that? Who was it?

It was then that Aqua smiled genially as she watched me squirm.

"It's fine, Kazuma; don't worry. As a goddess, a divine being, I don't think anything of seeing a mortal like you naked."

"Shut up! Don't smile there all goddess-like when you never actually act like one!"

…We'd defeated only one monster so far, but since there had been a death, the group decided to call it quits for the day.

The extermination quest was by volume—completely based on how many monsters we could slay.

The per-enemy rate was extraordinarily high, so when we'd first accepted the job, I'd thought it would be a piece of cake, but…

"Only…one?"

Karen's eyes widened at our report while we all sat in her drawing room.

"Yeah, one monster. Sorry we couldn't be of more help. However—"

Karen held up her hand as Darkness tried to speak.

"One monster? Even with the renowned Lady Dustiness, just a single creature?" she said mockingly and suddenly burst into laughter. "Ah-ha-ha-ha-ha-ha-ha. With all your big talk, that's the best you could do? The party with Axel's best adventurer, rumored to have defeated one of the Demon King's generals, and you couldn't do more than that?"

This woman was really getting on my nerves. Suddenly, the recipient of the noblewoman's abuse stood up.

"If you have something to say, then say it! I know you don't like me, but I'll be damned if I let you insult my companions!"

"I have tons to say! As the acting lord, you and your family put so many restrictions on lending that it's hurt profits! We were able to make plenty of money when Lord Alderp was in charge. Where did he go?!" Karen spoke insistently, standing up as well.

"Who asked for your opinion about me? I'm asking if you've got a problem with us killing one monster! Fine, though—if that's how you think, I'll settle this here! Lending is an important job, so I won't tell you to stop. But your interest is too high, and the way you hound people for money is disgusting."

"Girls like you are too ignorant and sheltered to understand. As long as people want to borrow at high interest, that makes it a consensual agreement. And you say we're too ruthless about collecting? When they come groveling to borrow money and then have the nerve to get mad about paying it back, what's wrong with squeezing it out of them?! People like that always ended up running off when Lord Alderp shouldered them with debt and forced them to marry him!"

Ah, even I know Karen just said something she shouldn't have.

"You have some nerve saying that, you lower noble! You'll pay for that. I'll kill you!"

"Y-you think you can? J-just try it, then! You're all talk anyway, Dustiness... Dustiness? Wait a minute, I'm no commoner. You'll be in big trouble if you harm me, you know?!"

"Neither the government nor its people would care if a crooked, upstart lender like you disappeared! For the sake of the world and its people, I'll get rid of you! There's no problem as long as I go quietly to jail or wherever... What, Megumin? Don't stop me. I'm going to deliver justice to this punk."

Karen was on the verge of tears while Darkness grabbed her. Megumin had interrupted by tugging gently on the blond woman's mantle.

"Darkness, that's enough. We basically failed the quest, after all. Kazuma's only just recovered, so why don't we go home?" Megumin, normally the most short-tempered of all, muttered quietly.

5

That night.

Collecting one monster's worth of pay from our now-very-flustered employer, we went straight back to the mansion and were relaxing after dinner.

Megumin said she had something to discuss with everyone. The explanation was a bit...

"...Sorry, can you start from the beginning again?"

"Well, I guess... Ummm, I formed a crew of bandits on a whim, but by the time I knew it, I had over a thousand applicants. Once I'd made the best manor in town our hideout and obtained some supporters, it was the perfect time to go raid a noble's home—that Karen girl's."

My body stiffened unconsciously.

What does she think she's doing?

Darkness, who was similarly frozen, looked about nervously and spoke. "Now that you mention it, I did hear someone had gotten their hands on the best mansion in town..."

Stop it.

"Yes, my grunt flaunted a bit of her power, and we were granted use of it."

"Hold up. I'm sure even the power of the Dustiness family couldn't snag that manor so easily. Hey, Megumin, might that grunt of yours be…?"

Hey, stop, don't ask that—there won't be any going back.

"Speaking of, Megumin, on the way to Elroad, you were calling that Iris girl your grunt, weren't you?"

"Stop it, Aqua. This is no time for an utter dimwit to be asking such questions! We heard nothing and know nothing. Got it?"

"Don't be ridiculous! C'mon—what's this about? Did you rope Lady Iris into a shady group and attack Karen's mansion with a bunch of weirdos you met somewhere?!" Darkness asked, dripping sweat and looking ready to cry.

"'Bunch of weirdos' is a rude way to put it. It was an ignorant grunt and a friendless Crimson Magic Clan member, plus an Axis priestess and one Thief—everyone else's enrollment is on hold for now."

I probably knew everyone except for the Thief she'd mentioned at the end.

Why did my companions always go and get themselves into trouble the moment I took my eyes off them?

"Besides, technically we just went to her home *planning* to raid it—we didn't get to execute the plan. I told you about this the other day, didn't I, Kazuma? That we helped the people at the mansion by killing the monsters attacking them."

I felt just a tiny bit relieved at Megumin's words.

No, there were lots of questions still in need of answering.

"Still, why did you make such a dumb group? Why can't you lead a more peaceful life?"

Despite the question being as sincere as I could muster, Megumin looked at me like she didn't understand at all.

"You should know that already. I will never forget—it was the day we all got to eat speckled crab again. While everyone was stuffing their faces, I gushed about how I'd met the Silver-Haired Thief Brigade, and how I admired them and their way of life. That's the reason I assembled my crew."

At this point, I couldn't admit I had been too engrossed in eating crab to listen to anything she'd been saying.

"And though I did not explain at the time that I'd made a thief gang, I told you I had gotten people together and acquired a hideout in Axel and that we had found some work, right?"

"Y-yeah, you did...of course...?"

Seeing Darkness looking around nervously, I was convinced she'd been too into the food to listen, either.

Jittery myself, I also glanced about the room. Next to me, Aqua was scratching her head.

"Sorry, I was too into the crab to hear what you were saying," came her shameless response.

...Are Darkness and I on the same level as this girl?

"...So after you helped her, you didn't even get a thank-you, much less a reward?" I asked to make sure I understood, after hearing about all the trouble with the noble girl.

"Yes, the reason that Karen girl was surprised to see me must have been because she remembered the time before and felt awkward about it. It would have been one thing if I had helped as a passerby, but I really only came to their aid after I went there to raid and saw monsters attacking..." Megumin hunched down, embarrassed.

"You felt too guilty to be pushy about money and left?"

"Yes..."

At my final question, the Arch-wizard dropped her shoulders dejectedly, likely reflecting on what had happened.

Megumin herself probably didn't want the money that much. She seemed to be worried about getting stiffed on payment in front of the other members of her gang, however.

Darkness had been listening quietly but suddenly opened her eyes wide and stood up.

"That stingy, sly little upstart! I can handle her making a mockery of Kazuma or me, but I definitely can't forgive a noble for running off a youngster like Megumin. She didn't even thank her!"

"H-hey, I understand what you're saying, but why are you fine with her bad-mouthing me?"

Darkness narrowed her eyes, clearly hearing what I had asked.

"Kazuma, we go tomorrow! Really, I wanna go right now, but tomorrow morning, we're getting everyone together for that raid! That's what Megumin had planned from the start, right? Now you have the approval of the Dustiness family—burn them to the ground!"

"Don't *you* say something dumb, too! Even our hotheaded Megumin thought better than to do that!"

"No, in my case, a pack of powerful monsters had appeared, so I just went along with my adventurer instincts instead of following the way of the bandit."

I wish you wouldn't sabotage me vouching for you!

"All of this is sounding pretty intense. I'll mind my own business and drink some booze so this doesn't get even more out of hand."

Why was this the one day Aqua seemed to be the most reasonable among us?

"Look out, Donnelly, 'cause I don't care what happens after! When everything's over, I won't fight a standing trial or whatever other consequences. I'll teach her a lesson!"

I fled back into my room after hearing Darkness give such a foreboding statement.

6

The area had grown totally dark, and the lights of the houses had vanished. There was a soft *knock-knock* at the door of my room.

"I'm awake!" I let them know it was okay to enter from my spot lying on the bed, and in came a small figure.

"Sorry to bother you so late."

It was Megumin.

Though she still hadn't changed into her pajamas despite the time—I imagined she had been feeling down ever since dinner. Yes, this girl had seemed to be somewhat depressed ever since my most recent resurrection.

She'd been pretending like nothing was wrong to keep us from noticing, but with how long I'd known her, that was basically impossible.

"What's wrong? You don't look like you're here for racy talk, and you don't seem like you're in a mood for jokes." I sat myself up as I spoke, knowing this wasn't the time to kid around.

Megumin's shoulders dropped, and her eyes turned to look at the floor.

"Sorry," came her soft apology.

"Er, I don't like how this sounds like a rejection. Especially after you came in here all of a sudden and only said one word."

I encouraged her to continue, and she did, though with her head still down.

"If I hadn't helped that noble earlier and instead raided their mansion as I should have, maybe you would not have died. After all, it is possible that Karen girl herself could be the cause of the monsters spawning around that house..." Megumin blurted out the words.

Huh?

Hadn't I heard something like that already?

Megumin continued on as I stayed silent.

"Their home might have a Sacred Treasure that summons monsters. If I had been able to steal it, that never would have happened to you—"

I interrupted her confession-like monologue, saying, "Who on earth did you hear that from?"

I was pretty sure I knew who it was already, though.

Not having expected me to ask for her source, even if I did say something, Megumin cast a crimson glance toward me in the dark.

"It was my crew's Thief, the one I talked about earlier. Um, it is someone you know, but..." There was a hint of a smile on the girl's face.

Sighing, I got out of bed and looked toward the window. They must have been deliberately thinking hostile thoughts, wanting me to notice them. The person in question was probably starting to get cold outside. For a while now, my Sense Foe skill had been telling me someone was waiting outside the window.

Megumin gave me an odd look as I suddenly rose and walked toward the window. I drew the curtains on the window with a *swish*, and…

"'Thief' means this person, right?" My words came as though I had known this was going to happen.

It was neither Eris the goddess nor Chris but rather the grunt from a knockoff crew of bandits who entered. Rather, the person waving from past the glass was my currently wanted boss, face covered with a mask.

7

"Phew. I swear, it takes you so long to notice, Lowly Assistant. I was getting really chilly."

Chris slipped inside when I opened the window for her.

"Well, you didn't set a time in the first place, did you, Chief? Though we should probably start holding these meetings outside," I replied, as if this was an everyday thing.

Megumin stood motionless, dumbfounded at our exchange.

"…Hey, Lowly Assistant, Megumin's not moving."

"Probably because of your unorthodox entrance, Chief. I mean, a suspicious person entering through an open window is pretty startling."

We grinned through our irreverent remarks. Of course, we knew the real reason Megumin had gone rigid.

"…rry."

"Hmm?"

"What's wrong, Megumin? I couldn't hear you."

After her soft murmur before, Megumin appeared to make up her mind about something and suddenly began to grovel on the floor.

"I am sorry! I cannot believe I, calling myself a fan, could not see who you really were!"

"H-hey, keep your voice down—people will hear you!" I warned.

"It's fine, it's fine, Megumin! It's not even worth apologizing for, so quit apologizing!"

As the two of us tried our best to hurriedly calm her down, Megumin raised her face and stared.

"Though, errr... You called him your lowly assistant a second ago, which means..."

Her red eyes were full of excitement and expectation, making me feel uneasy about playing dumb or evading the question. I looked at Chris, as if to ask if this was okay. She signaled back that it was, winking and giving a thumbs-up.

Chris had come in knowing Megumin was here, so she must've meant to reveal her identity.

In that case, I didn't need to hide who I was anymore, either.

I went to the closet where I kept my thieving clothes and mask...

"Megumin, watch veeery carefully and see the true identity of the person you told me you liked so fervently," Chris said teasingly. The silver-haired girl grinned like a mischievous kid while she stood next to the closet I'd opened.

Megumin replied, "Okay, I shall. I want to know what the person I like so much has been doing all this time, after all."

Megumin's counter had been a head-on fastball; Chris was the one to turn red.

"Chief, this one never pulls any punches, so you're better off not teasing her. I have taken hit after hit from her myself."

"S-s-s-sorry. I don't know what that was, but I'm feeling a lot of damage myself. What is this bittersweet feeling? I'm embarrassed yet want to hear more. Somehow, at the same time, there's an urge to cover my face..."

Taking stock of our hushed whispers, Megumin looked just a bit sad, saying, "Er, are you guys really close? How long have you two had this kind of relationship?"

"No, Megumin! We only recently started thieving together, and I told you before—I don't think anything of my lowly assistant! He's just a friend; I don't have any special feelings!"

"Wait a second—what have the two of you been talking about behind my back? Why have I been rejected without even knowing about it?"

What have these two really been talking about when I'm not around? I need to take care to make more inappropriate comments and actions; gotta keep them from holding their gossip conventions.

While I considered my actions for the future, I suddenly felt a powerful gaze from behind as I changed my clothes.

"I know we just talked about watching carefully and revealing my true identity, but surely this part is a bit..."

The two of them, staring at me with earnest faces, averted their eyes in panic as I put my hand to my pants.

"...A lovely full moon tonight! I know it doesn't matter for you and your Darksight skill, Lowly Assistant, but for me, nights like this are a great time to get to work."

Relying only on pale moonlight, we departed from Axel.

Megumin was wearing a rough getup rather than her usual robes. According to Chris, she'd gone to the trouble of getting a mask just for this.

"Er, is it really okay for me to come, too? I don't have any thief skills, so won't I slow you down?" Megumin had been following us from one step behind for a while.

"Don't worry. There's another person en route to help us out. Anyway, think of me as someone else behind this mask. I am not the masterful adventurer Kazuma Satou but the wanted boss of the Masked Thief Brigade. It only happens on full moons, but sometimes I get this feeling like I can never lose. And I'm definitely feeling it tonight!" This is what I said to the Crimson Magic Clanner who had joined us on that night.

"Hey, Lowly Assistant, you're not actually some sort of devil or demon, are you? Just a human, right? Also, it's the Silver-Haired Thief Brigade, and I'm the chief, got it?"

Ignoring the real boss's usual rudeness, I hurried on, only slightly bothered by the continuous watchful look from behind me.

After all, tomorrow, a big, raging noble was going to make a move practically at odds with Megumin. That blond woman was already stubborn enough, but once I'd seen her eyes so serious, I had given up on stopping her. Therefore, our only chance was to snatch the object that was supposedly summoning monsters from Karen's house—by morning.

If we could just steal the thing, it would hopefully be enough to keep Darkness at bay. Then we could have that girl tried lawfully for summoning harmful creatures and exposing Axel to danger.

Now that I thought about it, I was a victim myself, having been sent to meet Eris. I'd have nothing to complain about if we actually managed to pull this off.

...

"You know, I really can't stop feeling your eyes on me."

"Ah! S-s-sorry, the mask suits you so well, I just couldn't help it..."

Megumin had been staring at me nonstop while she followed the boss and me.

"Anyway, we'll arrive at the town gate soon, so you put on a mask, too, Megumin. Today, you're a member of the Silver-Haired Thief Brigade, you know."

At Chris's words, Megumin's eyes glowed red with excitement, and she covered her mouth with a mask.

"...This is bad, Chief—her red eyes make her mask practically worthless."

"What should we do, Lowly Assistant? I hadn't counted on this, either."

Even with a mask covering the lower half of her face, the distinguishing feature of the Crimson Magic Clan made it totally obvious who it was. This town had only two Crimson Magic Clan members, so the eyes were a dead giveaway.

I took off my mask and held it out to Megumin, who was unmistakably crestfallen.

"Oh well, wear my mask. I'll use yours. Tonight, you're the chief of the Masked Thief Brigade."

"Hey, Lowly Assistant, let's make sure we're on the same page about the name of our group. Also, I call the shots, okay?"

Megumin took the mask from me and smiled, happier than ever.

"When we got the bounty on our heads, didn't I tell you we should be the Masked Thief Brigade and that I should be in charge?"

"The buzz has died down recently, and I was the one who originally made the thief gang, so we have to name it after my trademark silver hair."

Such was our exchange as I donned the mask Megumin had handed me.

"I am good at coming up with names. If you like, I could name the gang?" the crimson-eyed girl offered.

""No,"" Chris and I accidentally said in unison.

…Getting through Axel's main gate was all too easy thanks to the Ambush skill; beneath the moonlight, we pressed on toward the forest.

"Kazuma, it somehow feels so right having this mask on. You might even say it suits a Crimson Magic Clan member more than anyone. Can I have this?"

"I've been getting fond of it recently myself, so I'm not giving it to you. Vanir's place is selling ones just like it, so buy one yourself. Apparently, they're so popular that it's hard to get one, though."

Listening, Chris asked curiously, "Is Vanir that guy who always wears a mask? I only caught a glimpse of him from afar, but he seemed to be an honest person. He was driving crows away from the trash heaps, getting called Crow Slayer and all that."

…What is she talking about? Are all the goddesses in this world blind?

No, as I recalled, he had said something about using a temporary body when coming down to the earth, so maybe that's why she didn't recognize Vanir?

Although it seemed extremely risky, I kind of wanted to introduce Chris to Wiz and Vanir.

"…Oh, I can see the mansion now. Well, Megumin, I guess tonight is your second chance. You were actually pretty mad about that girl's attitude, weren't you?" Chris said, smiling at Megumin, who stared at the forest manor with eyes shining from behind her mask.

"Well, let's go!"

8

Two sentries were standing nonchalantly at the front gate, apparently watching for monsters.

To get rid of them, I activated my Ambush skill and approached quietly from the darkness.

Covering their mouths from behind and using Drain Touch should work.

...Just then, there was a rustling sound opposite from where I had been sneaking, to the left of the guards.

The two watchmen, who had been facing the main gate, turned to look, and...

Not missing the opportunity, I approached their backs in an instant, put one hand around each of their mouths, and activated Drain Touch.

Seeing them crumple without a sound, Chris and Megumin emerged from where they were hiding in the brush.

"Well, both of you did great. Actually, you were even better than I expected, Kazuma."

Megumin, who seemingly thought I'd be terrible at this, looked at us with respect in her eyes. The sound that had distracted the sentries was a rock Chris had thrown.

"We are the Silver-Haired Thief Brigade, who broke into the heart of the king's palace, you know? Something like this is a piece of cake," Chris said with a grin, as if she had everything under control.

"You were the grunt of a knockoff group until just recently—what are you talking about? Anyway, why do things always get amusing when I'm not around, Chief?"

"That's what I want to know. My Luck is just as good as yours, after all."

Speaking of, Chris's words made me realize something. As good as my Luck was, I always, always got wrapped up in the darnedest things. I thought on that while we circled around the mansion grounds and broke in from the back entrance.

"...Hmm, maybe we aren't as lucky as we thought?"

"I feel like this isn't so much good luck as it is drawing the short stick."

"You two must have a lot of experience to be so calm at a time like this."

Exchanging looks, we tried to figure out how to deal with the situation we'd suddenly found ourselves in.

"I don't know who you are, but stop talking and help me!"

Karen stood before us, getting constricted by a human-size, octopus-like monster.

"...Th-thanks for the help. I almost lost my innocence as a young noble girl..."

After rescuing Karen and slicing up the octo-monster with Chris, we realized the room we'd entered was some kind of cage.

There was a door at the far end of the room, but in its middle, iron bars had been set up.

It was probably supposed to be a system for summoning monsters safely from the other side of the makeshift prison.

"Why is the back entrance connected to a jail?"

In response to my question, the recently constricted Karen stood up, clearing her throat in an awkward sort of way.

"That is no back entrance. It is an outlet for releasing unwanted monsters."

Only now did Karen look at us with any sort of caution; the noble-woman threateningly raised something in her hand up high.

"She said 'unwanted monsters' just now, Chief. This girl is totally guilty."

"Wait, Lowly Assistant. I don't see the all-important Sacred Treasure anywhere."

Showing slight annoyance at our calm composure, Karen broke into a shout.

"Who are you people?! You came in here knowing what this place is, didn't you?"

"The infamous Donnelly home, yes? We've come for payback," Chris said with confidence.

"I see. When in the lending business, you make no shortage of enemies. That's what you're saying, right? Unfortunately for you, you're all going to be test subjects for my new product!" Karen swung the object in her hand over her hand, and...!

""*Steal.*""

Chris and I used the skill simultaneously, and the object was plucked from Karen's hand.

"Wha—?!"

Ignoring Karen's yelp of surprise, we checked out our spoils of war.

"I just went ahead and stole it, but what exactly is this?"

"Ah, rats, I lost! Panties again!"

The item Karen had been trying to use had wound up in Chris's hands, while white underwear had fallen into mine.

"Why is your Steal specialized for sexual harassment, Kazuma? ... Anyway, let me see that for a second. I am sure I have seen it somewhere bef— No, not the panties. I mean that stone there!"

Chris gave the object in her hand to Megumin. Meanwhile, Karen held down the hem of her skirt, glaring at me as I wondered what to do with her underwear.

In the midst of that bizarre situation, Karen yelled, "S-somebody help! We have intruders, thieves!" finally thinking to call someone.

"This is a contraband magical item, processed from monster eggs. It can summon them, but that is all. Once conjured, there's no controlling them, and the summons are random—it's treasure, just a regular, dangerous item."

At Megumin's insight into what the stone really was, Karen snorted disdainfully.

"Regular? No, it is a wonderful tool for moneymaking. Among the randomly summoned monsters is the possibility of hitting the jackpot with a Duxion or a Gold Ant. The biggest hit I've had so far was a baby dragon. That alone made back everything I spent on these things in the first place."

Several sets of distant footsteps were growing closer. Karen, who had put some distance between herself and us, took a new stone from a shelf.

So basically, this girl was summoning monsters into this bar-covered room, selling off the ones that were worth anything, and carelessly releasing into the wild the ones that couldn't make her a profit.

Then, when rumors started to fly in town about the monsters, she had solicited help from me, famed as the strongest in Axel, to cull them.

"Chief, this girl is just a punk. She even blabs about her misdeeds."

"You shouldn't say such things even if you're thinking them. Still, this isn't the culprit. Just when I'd thought I found the one using the Sacred Treasure..."

"That lady can hear the two of you. Her face is bright red."

Furious at us, who spoke as casually as we always did, Karen readied the stone.

"You may feel quite at ease now, but you'll have plenty of time to regret your actions in the afterlife! The guards will be here any second—"

""*Steal.*""

Before Karen could finish, we both unleashed our skill again.

"That makes two wins."

"Now, hold on a minute. In my mind, I'm happier with this than that stone, so if we're making it a contest, I count this as a win for me."

"This boy is vile; he came right out and said such a thing right in front of us."

Clutched in my hands was Karen's bra, while Chris had snagged the stone.

"What kind of people are you?! Seriously, what's with you two?!"

Karen gave a tearful glare as she now held down her neckline in addition to her skirt.

That's when…

"Milady, what's wrong?!"

"Intruders! Seize these people!" Karen ordered triumphantly to the guards who had arrived.

…Chris turned to us, the others on this side of the bars, and said, "Lowly Assistant, this person is kind of a lost cause."

"We already knew she wasn't worth it to begin with. I mean, she's like someone who buys loot boxes in a mobile game with this contraband."

"What are 'loot boxes in a mobile game'?" Megumin asked. "Anyway, I wonder why she was summoning monsters on her side of the bars. I bet this lady was organizing the shelves or something and dropped that stone, causing a monster to come out."

As Karen turned bright red up to her ears at what we'd said, Chris nodded in agreement.

"We just got here, but maybe this is our chance? We'll take this as evidence of illegal monster summoning. Let's report it to the Dustiness family."

Hearing that, Karen's face went from red to pale.

"W-wait! I won't let you go. I may not look it, but I am a high-level noble myself. I can buy time until the guards make their way around back—"

"*Stea—*"

"No, sidekick, I don't think you should do that anymore!"

When I tried to use a certain skill on Karen again, Chris was quick to interrupt.

"I see no problem. Let us leave this girl stark naked in front of her own servants."

At Megumin's merciless words, Karen, who knew what was about to happen to her and her one-piece, sank to the floor and backed away, trembling.

I figured it was time to quit while I was ahead; we'd gotten the evidence. As Chris had said, it was probably time to withdraw.

Seeming to pick up on who we were, Karen spoke from where she was on the floor.

*   *   *

"Now that I've gotten a good look, that mask seems familiar. You're the Masked Thief Brigade people are talking about, aren't you?! Little illegal items like these aren't enough to ruin my family. Just you wait—you're going to get an even bigger bounty on your heads… Just kidding. I'm sorry!"

Karen quickly retracted her words and backed away when she saw me thrust my hand toward her.

Epilogue

The next morning.

"Ha-ha-ha-ha-ha-ha-ha! Ha-ha-ha-ha-ha-ha-ha-ha! I'll teach you a lesson with this, you Donnelly jerk! Good job, Kazuma! Well done! Ha-ha-ha-ha-ha-ha-ha-ha-ha-ha!"

Darkness's triumphant laughter echoed through the foyer. Having obtained evidence of monster summoning, I bestowed it upon Darkness and gave a rough explanation of what had transpired the night before.

Though she did scold us a bit for breaking in, ultimately her reaction was pretty positive.

"G'morning… What's going on, everyone? You're up early today."

Aqua came down in her pajamas, holding some kind of bundle.

"Not up early—we stayed up all night. I'm going to sleep now, so don't wake me till evening," I said.

"Were you gaming again? Sheesh, these NEETs, for the love of…"

I didn't wanna hear it from a girl who had drunk booze and slept through all the commotion of last night.

And then Aqua spread out her bundle on the table, at which Megumin showed interest.

"What are those, Aqua? They look like stones."

"Just as I'd expect from a member of the Crimson Magic Clan, Megumin, you have an eye for appraisal."

That eye is as blind as a bat—she never noticed who I really was beneath my mask until yesterday.

I sipped my morning coffee while Aqua continued.

"This here is a collection of funny-shaped stones. You can find some good ones in rivers, ponds, and lakes. I polish them to a shine like this sometimes... Want one?"

"I do not," Megumin answered.

...Although the monster-summoning commotion was over, the missing Sacred Treasure hadn't been at the mansion, so Chris had decided to keep working on tracking down its whereabouts.

I really wanted to make this goddess, who could never keep her big mouth shut, learn from the more diligent one.

"Speaking of, Aqua, you've been heading in and out of town for a while now—what is it you're doing? When we took our eyes off Megumin, everything got out of hand by the time we knew it. I'm just as curious what you were up to..."

"Darkness, stop treating me like a problem child! Someone at the Adventurers Guild asked me to do a part-time job. Look, I have super-amazing Purification magic, right? They asked me to use that to purify the lake and the area surrounding where the Kowloon Hydra used to be. I really gave it my best!"

I took another slow drink of coffee, absentmindedly watching an all-too-familiar scene. Megumin was standing next to me, clutching something to her chest. She seemed to want to speak, but it looked like the girl was unsure whether it was a good idea.

"S-sorry, Aqua. My bad."

"Do you really think it's your fault? Then buy something from my stone collection. With the Purification job over, I've got no money."

Ignoring their prattle, I teasingly said to Megumin, "Is there something you wanna say? Aha, do you want my autograph now that you know who I really am? Or maybe you want me to shake your hand?"

"I do not."

After I looked about nervously for a bit at her scathingly immediate

answer, she said, "…Er, thank you very much. For sort of getting revenge for us."

Oh, that?

"It wasn't exactly revenge. Besides, it was that noble girl's fault I got killed. So it was a bit satisfying for me, personally. You guys are our subsidiaries anyway, right? In that case, it's only natural to get revenge for a grunt."

While I put on airs, Megumin bashfully said, "Well, from now on, shall I call you 'boss,' Kazuma?"

"Sure, I don't mind. The bounty lists our name as the 'Masked Thief Brigade.' So you could say I'm the boss… Oh, don't tell Chris I said that, okay? She'll get mad."

Megumin giggled gleefully at my slight panic.

"Fine. I will keep it a secret, so if I do that for you…"

She gripped the thing she was clutching to her chest tightly for a second.

"Just on occasion, can I come along again?"

As she spoke, she held out what she had apparently been clutching for so long—my mask.

Afterword

Thank you very much for purchasing *Konosuba: An Explosion on This Wonderful World! Bonus Story: We Are the Megumin Bandits.*

I doubt this is the first *Konosuba* book anyone has read, but I am *Some-Authorlike-Nickname*, aka Natsume Akatsuki.

This book is a spin-off novel that was serialized on Sneaker Web, to which I added text that was previously unpublished.

I already explained how this came to be written in the afterword of *Konosuba*'s tenth volume, so I will spare you that, but I sure learned this isn't something to do on a whim.

I earnestly pray there will never be another character popularity vote.

…Anyway, this volume is a book packed with various untold stories.

Even that Sacred Treasure, which Chris is still hunting for after chucking it in the lake at the end of Volume 7, was picked up by the goddess with a reputation for doing the uncalled for. She polishes it every day without having a clue what it actually is.

Surely Chris will collapse when she probably ends up finding it at Kazuma and company's mansion, after having searched high and low for it everywhere.

If I get the opportunity, I'd like to write such a story sometime, too.

…Well then, by the time this hits the bookstores, the anime should be approaching its second season.

I haven't been able to show up much for the anime's post-recording this time, either, but an author is an animal that makes its habitat indoors, so it can't be helped!

I get spoiled hard when I go to recordings, so I try not to take part—instead, I'm looking forward to the second anime season as a regular anime fan myself.

Also, next month an art book by the masterful Kurone Mishima called *Cheers!* will go on sale.

I wrote a special story just for that, too, so if anyone is interested, then please do not hesitate to check it out.

I would be happy if you enjoyed the manga, as well, which is being serialized in many magazines.

Well then, as with previous volumes, I would like to thank first the masterful Kurone Mishima, as well as the many people who helped make this publication possible.

And most of all, I once again express my deep appreciation for all the readers who picked up this book!

Natsume Akatsuki

A Hardworking Girl Thief

I ran into an unusual pair as I was strolling around town.

"The Axis Church! Please join the Axis Church!"

It was Cecily, shouting the praises of her religion.

Joining her was…

"The Axis Church… Please join the Axis Church…"

Chris was clutching a ton of applications—perhaps forced to do so by Cecily—and was handing them out with a look of resignation.

"Er, what are you doing?"

When I spoke to them, Chris jumped as if she'd been caught doing something bad.

"Ahhh, Megumin! We're doing some PR, of course! I was just looking for more hands—won't you help? As thanks, I'll treat you to lunch!"

"I don't mind doing it for a bit, but why is an Eris follower like Chris part of this, too?"

The Thief looked embarrassed by my question but nevertheless held out an application to a passerby, saying, "When I was bored and went to spend time at the hideout, Cecily said to me, 'The Axis Church feels inferior now, thanks to the goddess Eris gracing everyone with an appearance so freely before. Isn't your goddess a little too thoughtless?' Then she asked me to help out for just today to show that I felt even a little sorry for them…"

Why is this person such a pushover?

"Axis followers' complaints are fundamentally flawed, so you shouldn't do what they tell you to. Eris deciding to come down and create confusion doesn't have anything to do with a believer like you, right?"

"I—I think I'd better help out all day."

I wasn't sure why she said that, but if it was fine with her, then oh well.

"Well, what should I help with? Shoving applications into everyone's mailboxes or something?"

A smile made its way across Cecily's face after my question.

"No, since you're here, Megumin, let's finally do you-know-what again!"

...On Axel's main street.

Loudly, I cried to the passing people for assistance.

"Please, won't someone help me?! My pet cat is on the verge of death after a passing Eris follower attacked her!"

I was cradling Chomusuke—who had been brushing up happily against my legs—with both hands to prevent her from struggling.

With eyes glazed over like she'd given up on everything, Chris said to me, "M-my Eris-follower senses tell me that cat is eviiil. All I did was exact justice in the name of my goddess, so I'm not sooorry. If you really want to save her, you'll have to join the Eris Chuuurch."

Chris's monotone speech was the cue for Cecily to appear; the priestess pushed her way through the onlookers.

"That's enough, wicked Eris follower! Persecuting a poor little girl's pet cat in a scheme to get her to make a big donation to the Eris Church if she wants you to heal its wounds? Even if a police officer was to forgive you, Lady Aqua and I cannot!"

The people around us whispered to one another upon seeing our little play.

"Isn't that Megumin from Kazuma's place? Is this some kind of new game of hers?"

"Chris too—what is she doing? She seemed like such a respectable young woman…"

"Hey, don't look them in the eye. They'll try to talk to you."

Hearing that, Chris covered her face with both hands and collapsed. Apparently, she couldn't take it anymore.

"Just great, you and Chris are so famous that I can't use the usual trick! There goes my perfect plan, where a beautiful priestess revives the kitten with a miraculous Heal, and you're so moved that you join the Axis Church in tears. Then the onlookers are lured into becoming believers one after another…"

"I said I would help, not that I would join! Besides, I cannot do acting *that* advanced!"

And just then.

Suddenly feeling a presence behind me, I turned around, and…

"What're you doing?"

Kazuma and Darkness were standing there; they'd gone out to buy dinner.

The two of them had most interesting expressions on their faces. They looked on at Chris with pity in their eyes.

"N-n-n-no, Darkness! Listen, Lowly Assistant! This is my apology to the Axis followers for the inconvenience they suffered when Eris appeared or something like that…!"

Darkness placed a kind hand on Chris's shoulder while the poor girl made a panicked excuse. Next to her, Kazuma grinned.

"Chris…," Darkness started. "If there's ever anything that's troubling you, I'm here to listen, okay? You can lean on me a bit more instead of doing something this dumb…"

"Er, if there's anything I can do, I'll help, too. I'd rather you not lower the number of people around here with common sense. It's low enough as it is."

"No! Both of you, this isn't what you think! I'm begging you; stop looking at me like that!!"